She sure surprised him

What struck Raney as most unusual was that Carol turned out to be just as good company as his buddies. Another thing was, she looked good. He had never really noticed it before, but outdoors she looked real good. Of course, he realized that consuming whiskey while being pressed up to her for an hour and a half just might be clouding his thinking. That and the fact that she was one of the few available women around. He was beginning to think it didn't matter if she wasn't his type. Anyway, it might be kind of interesting to get to know a Northerner....

Maybe he'd see about taking her out tonight. Only this time he'd get her to dance, not shoot pool. And if things felt right on the dance floor, who knew how the evening might end?

ABOUT THE AUTHOR

Beverly Sommers likes living alone, traveling alone, neon palm trees and red furniture.

Books by Beverly Sommers

HARLEQUIN AMERICAN ROMANCE
11—CITY LIFE, CITY LOVE
26—UNSCHEDULED LOVE
62—VERDICT OF LOVE
69—THE LAST KEY
85—MIX AND MATCH
125—CHANGING PLACES

HARLEQUIN INTRIGUE
3—MISTAKEN IDENTITY

HARLEQUIN AMERICAN ROMANCE
PREMIER EDITION
3—RIDE A PAINTED PONY

These books may be available at your local bookseller.

Don't miss any of our special offers. Write to us at the following address for information on our newest releases.

Harlequin Reader Service
P.O. Box 52040, Phoenix, AZ 85072-2040
Canadian address: P.O. Box 2800, Postal Station A,
5170 Yonge St., Willowdale, Ont. M2N 6J3

Changing Places

BEVERLY SOMMERS

Harlequin Books

TORONTO • NEW YORK • LONDON
AMSTERDAM • PARIS • SYDNEY • HAMBURG
STOCKHOLM • ATHENS • TOKYO • MILAN

This is for Phyllis Tornetta:
agent, confidante and fellow conspirator.

—————————•••—————————

Published November 1985

First printing September 1985

ISBN 0-373-16125-5

Chapter One

Interested in exchanging self-contained cabin in rural Georgia for furnished New York apartment for a minimum of six months. Contact J. J. Rafferty, RFD, Rock Ridge, Ga.

Carol had known for some time that she was growing tired of New York. She had been there eight years, and the thrill of being in the city had worn off. But if she gave up her rent-controlled apartment and then changed her mind and wanted to return to New York, she would probably have to pay three times as much rent for half the space, and she found she wasn't ready to take that chance.

There were three apartment exchanges listed in the *Voice* that week. One was for San Francisco, and that was tempting with winter approaching. But San Francisco was another city, not all that different from New York. Smaller, no doubt cleaner, but still a city.

The second one was for a condo on the beach in St. Thomas. The beach sounded pretty good, but the person advertising was quite specific about wanting to exchange for an apartment in the Village, which left Carol out.

The third one, the one about the cabin, held a certain appeal. Still, she didn't know a thing about Georgia, about the entire South for that matter. Nor was it a place she had ever been curious about. So she didn't give it any serious consideration until she found herself sketching pictures of log cabins when she should have been working.

And then she began fantasizing about living in a cabin in a rural area of the South. She was aware she was romanticizing the idea out of all proportion to reality, but she couldn't seem to let go of it.

She would walk out into the noisy, jostling, noon-day crowds of New York and find herself picturing woods and streams and wildlife and quiet country roads with no traffic.

She would be shoved on the sidewalk or be ignored by salespeople, and her mind would envision simple country people, the kind who would wish you good-morning on the street and greet you by name in the stores.

She would be awakened in the middle of the night by sirens or street fighting, and she would wonder what it would be like to wake up to the sound of birds singing.

It was getting so that she had to unplug the phone while working in order to get a stretch of unbroken time, and when she did pick it up, it was generally someone she had no interest in talking to.

And then one day, just out of curiosity, she wrote Mr. J. J. Rafferty a letter describing her apartment and expressing an interest in an exchange.

Ten days later she received a charming letter in return, which was followed by several phone calls.

And then she mentioned it to her friends, and they all told her she was crazy. They said that to begin with, she would hate it in the South, that even the rural sections of Vermont would probably drive her up the wall. They told her she would be bored out of her skull, that she'd be back in a month.

Carol told her agent about her idea, but unlike her friends, Phyllis was supportive. "Sure, you could use a rest," she was told. "Maybe the change will be good for you, give you some new ideas. You don't need to be in New York all the time—that's what you've got an agent for."

And Carol, who wouldn't have described herself as impulsive, took the plunge.

"YOU UNDERSTAND," Carol had told Mr. Rafferty after showing him through the apartment and exchanging keys, "it's conceivable I might hate it down there and want to return sooner. Of course a deal's a deal—I wouldn't throw you out of here."

J. J. Rafferty, who was far older than he had sounded over the telephone—close to seventy, she surmised—nodded his head. "Miss Jones, I'm not tied down to any time limit on this. If you really hate it, just give me a call."

"I mean, I like the idea of it. Peace, quiet, no crowded stores, no muggings..." Carol broke off the litany, not wanting to scare him off. "Mostly, I guess, I'm looking for solitude."

In his accented voice she had trouble understanding, he said, "Unhappy love affair?"

She gave him a look of surprise. "These days it's an accomplishment in New York to have any kind of love affair. The men are outnumbered and extremely wary." She stopped, not wanting to bore him with the life-style of the average New Yorker. He probably wouldn't understand, anyway. "I really just felt like a change," she told him, "and when I saw your ad in the *Voice*, it sounded perfect."

He stood looking out the doors to the terrace for a moment, then turned and surveyed her large living room. "I better warn you. I could fit my cabin into this room and have space left over."

"I don't care about that," Carol assured him. "Anyway, I don't have six acres and a stream."

Before she left, he gave her a detailed map he had drawn, directing her to Rock Ridge, along with the name of his nearest neighbor, and she made out a list for him of where to shop for groceries and where the nearest laundry and library were.

Then he surprised her. "I think I can find my way around," he told her. "I lived here for a couple of years when I was in my early twenties."

"Why did you leave?"

There was a self-mocking tone to his voice when he said, "Oh, in those days I thought a writer had to be in either Greenwich Village or Paris. I finally found out that in order to really write, you better stay away from both."

He had already told her he was a short-story writer, but since she had been embarrassed at never hearing of him, she had changed the subject.

"So what made you decide to come back now?" she asked.

"I just wanted to see it once more before I die." She must have looked shocked, because he smiled then and said, "Dont worry. I don't think I'm going to die on you in your pretty apartment. But I'm pushing eighty-six; I'm not going to live forever."

Carol couldn't do anything but just look at him in amazement.

SHE THOUGHT of that now as she parked her car in front of the cabin and sat looking around in similar amazement at the setting. Not that most of the drive down hadn't been equally pretty, but there seemed to be something special about this particular cabin and the woody area surrounding it.

Partly it was the season, of course. It was late October, and the trees were all turning, something she only caught occasional glimpses of in New York, and then usually when she was driving past Central Park in a taxi. The cabin, standing in stark simplicity in its clearing, was as small as he had warned her but perfectly proportioned and built authentically of logs. A center door, a window on each side, a chimney on the left—the whole thing looked like a picture out of one of her history books when she had been a child.

She couldn't help the sense of adventure, the feeling of new beginnings, as she got out of her car and walked up to the door. She turned the key in the lock, pushed the door open and felt the chill air as she stepped inside. On the telephone he had told her it was heated only by the fireplace but that there was electricity.

The surrounding trees shaded the cabin, but there was enough daylight left that she could see. What caught her eye first was one entire wall covered with bookcases and stuffed to capacity with books. That solved the problem of reading material, a necessity, since there was no television.

A worn couch and two end tables with good reading lamps stood along the front wall to her left. The back wall had been partitioned off, and one look through the door showed her a small bathroom with a stall shower and a toilet, but no sink, and next to that the one closet where a red-and-black-checked wool shirt still hung. The right wall held a small refrigerator, a sink and a counter on which sat a toaster oven and a hot plate. Two open shelves above held a motley assortment of dishes and cooking utensils. Below the right front window were a wooden table and two chairs. The only unutilized space was at the left wall in front of the fireplace, which would be perfect for her drawing table. She saw with relief that stacks of logs sat next to the fireplace; Mr. Rafferty had also told her there were more in the rear of the cabin. Then she saw something that surprised her. Hanging on the wall over the fireplace was some kind of rifle. Mr. Rafferty hadn't seemed the type to have guns in his house, but then she really hadn't got to know him all that well.

Carol stood in the center of the cabin on the bare wood floor and turned slowly around, viewing it all, not able to stop smiling at the perfection of it. If she had made a drawing of the perfect cabin, she couldn't have done better. Oh, she would need a few things, a few personal touches to make it her own, but she would make sure they were things that would fit in, things that Mr. Rafferty wouldn't resent upon his return and might even get enjoyment out of.

Going back outside, she opened the trunk of the car and took out her folding drawing table and carried it inside, then returned for her stool and art materials. She took time setting it all up to the side of the fireplace, then returned to the car for her two duffel bags of clothes in the back seat.

The one closet wasn't going to begin to contain all her clothes, but then she had had to pack enough for a full year as well as leave Mr. Rafferty some closet space in New York. She put the bagful of summer clothes on the floor of the closet, then hung up only the winter clothes that she would need right away. In order to hang up more, she'd have to buy some hangers. Underwear and sweaters she arranged on the closet shelf until she got herself some kind of chest of drawers.

She found a jar half filled with instant coffee and put water to boil on the hot plate, then checked out the refrigerator. There were a half dozen eggs, some bacon, a container of margarine and, in the freezer compartment, half a loaf of bread. All of which would do for dinner and meant she wouldn't have to go shopping until the next day.

All in all, she was pretty pleased with the exchange. The cabin would be so easy to take care of it would be like playing house as a child. The view of the woods out the windows was everything she had hoped for, although it might not be a bad idea to put up some curtains. She didn't figure there would be other people around to look in, but she wasn't going to count on it.

It was kind of like starting her life all over, and she liked that idea.

RANEY CATLIN was on his way home from honky-tonking in the local gin mill, with nothing more on his mind than the fact that two of his buddies were infuriated with him for sweet-talking their wives, when he noticed the lights on in old J.J.'s cabin. He'd had a few too many, enough so that his truck was weaving slightly on the road but not so much that he couldn't remember taking J.J. to the train station just the other day. And the fact that J.J. told him he wasn't going to return for maybe as long as six months to a year.

There was something else he felt he should remember but couldn't. Was it something about looking out for the cabin? It could've been; he just couldn't rightly recall.

He slowed down, came to a stop, then backed up the road for a closer look. And in the process almost backed into a tree. He could just make out the shape of a car in front of the cabin, and that made no sense at all. J.J. didn't have a car; he didn't believe in them. He had walked everywhere his whole life, as far as Raney knew.

All the concentration he was doing was making him sober up, a fact he regretted. He liked going home with a buzz on, which usually put him right to sleep. Wait a minute. J.J. had said something—was it about someone using his cabin? Something like that. He hadn't told Raney to look out for the cabin; rather, that he should be of help if the person staying there needed it. The trouble was, Raney hadn't been paying much attention to anything J.J. had said, because J.J. had a tendency to ramble on, on just about any subject, and Raney usually just tuned him out. Not that J.J. couldn't be interesting; it wasn't that. It was just that he'd get hold of a subject and then never let it go. It was tiring, was all.

Raney turned off the motor and got out of the truck. Hell, now he was perfectly sober. He started walking toward the car, found that he wasn't absolutely sober, after all, and felt a little relieved. Perfectly sober wasn't any state to be in at eleven o'clock at night.

He leaned down to take a good look at the license plate and from the light out of the cabin window was able to see clearly the New York plates, which were a definite affront to his sensibilities. J.J. was letting a Yankee use his cabin? A damn northerner was now abiding in Rock Ridge? The old man had finally lost his marbles, all right, and it was going to be Rock Ridge that suffered the consequences. Damn! A Yankee. He couldn't rightly believe it.

Curious now and a little angry, he went up to the window and looked inside. Other than a duffel bag on the floor, the place appeared to be empty. Then the bathroom door opened, and a woman came out, causing Raney to back up a couple of feet so as not to be seen. Her head was wrapped in a towel, and she was wearing a long yellow robe made of some fuzzy material. Even with the bulky robe on, though, he could tell she was small. He couldn't abide small women. Small women always acted cute and usually had the personalities of high-school cheerleaders. Moreover, when he took a woman to bed, he liked a little warmth, and small women were invariably cold.

Her face was small, too. Small featured, nothing spectacular. Kind of washed-out looking, as though she'd just taken her makeup off. He looked down at her bare feet and took note of the fact that she didn't even paint her toenails. Then she looked up and seemed to be staring directly at him, and he froze to the spot and stopped breathing. Just what he needed, to be taken for some kind of Peeping Tom. At least she was wearing a robe. If she had walked out stark naked, he would really have felt like the worst kind of voyeur. And rightly so, too.

Well, she didn't look as if she needed any looking after, and she probably wouldn't appreciate his just knocking on the door when she was fixing for bed, anyway. When she finally went over to the fireplace and lifted up a log, he quickly turned around and beat it back to his truck. He'd stop by again over the weekend and see if she was getting along all right. It was the least he could do for old J.J., especially since he was sure he'd been asked and was her nearest neighbor and all.

He still couldn't understand why J.J. had let his cabin to a New Yorker. And a woman at that. He couldn't even figure why a woman would want to live in J.J.'s cabin. Hell, she wouldn't know the first thing about taking care of herself out in the woods. Probably one of those fast-talking, sophisticated types. Comes down in her Mercedes, probably sporting a mink coat, thinking it would be fun to rough it for a while. He'd give her a month, maybe not even that long, and he bet she'd be hightailing it back to the city. Her kind didn't belong down here.

A damn Yankee! Just the thought of it made him want to head back to the Voyager and get drunk all over again.

WILLIE CATLIN, age fifteen, heard his father come into the house, stumble over the throw rug in the hall, then let out a stream of curses. Willie feigned sleep and hoped his father had been too drunk to notice the dent in the side of the jeep. Not that he wouldn't notice it eventually, but he'd rather have the confrontation when his father was sober.

Not that he saw Raney sober too often. He was pretty sure he didn't drink on the job, and he had never seen his father take a drink first thing in the morning, but nights and weekends were a whole other story. He had a temper when he got drunk, too; he sometimes got mean and wanted to start fights. Willie preferred to avoid him at those times.

After just a couple of drinks his father was great. At that stage he was kind of cheery, usually told him a few jokes, gave him a few bucks whether he needed it

or not and sometimes took him down to the Mc-
Donald's on the highway for dinner. But after the first
couple of drinks, watch out.

He heard the footsteps on the stairs and knew he
would find out in a matter of seconds just how much
Raney was noticing that night. Trying to make his
breathing even, although that had never helped before, Willie vowed to keep silent this time and not say
anything that might further antagonize his father.
That was hard to do, though; he guessed he took after
Raney in that respect. Neither was particularly noted
for being closemouthed, which got Raney in trouble
at bars and Willie in trouble at school.

Moments later, the ceiling light in Willie's bedroom
was switched on, which was a sure sign his father had
noticed, all right. Despite his efforts to breathe slowly
and evenly, Willie found himself holding his breath.

Raney, his speech only slightly slurred, said, "Who
gave you permission to use the jeep, boy?"

Willie pretended to stir in his sleep, then turned over
on his side to face the doorway. Very slowly, he opened
his eyes, blinked a little, then said a slow "What?"

"Don't go trying to fool me, Willie, 'cause you
know you can't. You think I don't remember where I
parked the jeep? You think I'm going to believe it just
somehow up and moved itself a few yards?"

Willie breathed a sigh of relief. At least he hadn't
noticed the dent. Maybe he could get Bubba down at
the garage to fix it for him before it was noticed.
"Only drove it down the road and back. I need practice, Dad, and you never go out with me."

"Know old J.J.'s cabin?"

The switch in subject matter threw Willie. He just couldn't figure out what J.J.'s cabin had to do with anything. He slid himself up in bed and blinked some more. His dad seemed to be waiting for an answer, though, so he finally said, "Yeah, sure I know it. Been by it about a million times, haven't I?" Wising off, as usual, but it had been a stupid question.

"Want you to go by there tomorrow after school."

"What for?"

"Some New York lady's staying there. Told J.J. I'd look in on her, see if there was anything she needed."

"Yeah, sure, I'll stop by." He was relieved that his dad wanted a favor from him and wasn't going to say anything more about the jeep.

"Good. See that you do," said Raney, then turned the light back off and went down the hall to his own room.

Willie couldn't figure out why a New York lady would be staying in J.J.'s cabin, but he didn't mind checking it out. He couldn't remember ever seeing a New Yorker in person. J.J. probably knew all kinds of strange people, though; he'd heard that J.J. had traveled some when he was young. Course that was centuries ago, but he'd probably met some strange people.

Maybe he could even pick up a few bucks helping her out. She'd probably need firewood cut and all kinds of things. But before he went and helped her out, he'd try to do something about that dent in the jeep. Except it would take money, and money was something he never seemed to have enough of.

Well, maybe the New York lady would change all that.

CAROL LAY IN BED and couldn't sleep. It was the quiet. She kept waiting to hear some sound, some audible evidence that she wasn't the only person left in the world. She didn't expect sirens where she was or the sounds of street fighting or even the rumble of a subway. But weren't there birds around? Didn't anybody have a dog that barked? Wasn't there wildlife around?

It was unnerving.

She finally switched on the lamp and looked at her watch. One-thirty, which meant she'd been trying to sleep for a good hour to no avail. Still, the problem was no doubt the hour. It was her habit to stay up working until four, then sleep until noon. She guessed she just wasn't used to going to bed so early.

She was hoping to break that habit down here, though. She had envisioned getting up with the sun, taking long early-morning walks through the woods, then returning to the cabin to work. Well, it would undoubtedly take time to ease into new hours. And she'd probably had too many cups of coffee that evening, too.

Restless, she got up out of the sofa bed, turned on all the lights and sat down at her drawing table. Not that working was going to put her to sleep; that was about the last thing it did. Instead, she could generally get so engrossed in her work that she lost all sense of time. It wasn't unusual for her to work until the sun came up, only the growing light in the room reminding her that so much time had passed.

It didn't bother Carol unduly that her work was the most important thing in her life, that in fact she often used it as an excuse to get out of socializing. Her love for her work paid her back in dividends: a sense of accomplishment, a feeling that she was creating and a burgeoning bank account that allowed her some of the luxuries of life.

Just to amuse herself, she picked up a felt-tip pen and began sketching a picture of a young black boy sleeping out on a fire escape. His face had a look of total concentration as he counted subway cars in his head in order to go to sleep. When she finished with the quick drawing, she wrote below it: You know you're getting old when you don't drop off fast anymore. Happy birthday.

Almost from the start Carol had been able to support herself with her drawings for one of the major greeting-card companies, but from the time she had instituted her series of street kids, the cards had really taken off. Now, with a line of stationery and calendars, as well as Christmas cards and regular greeting cards, she was, for the first time, making more money than she could easily spend. Also, a line of stuffed dolls of the street kids was due on the market before Christmas, and her agent had hopes that they would meet with some of the same success as the Cabbage Patch dolls.

Still wide awake, Carol looked through the books in the cases, finally taking out a worn volume called *Country Ramblings,* written by J. J. Rafferty.

She put another log on the fire, then got back in the sofa bed. The copyright in the book said it was published in 1941, and it was dedicated, with love, to someone named Elizabeth Ann.

Bored at the best of times by short stories, Carol was sure the dated book about country people would soon put her to sleep, but she was surprised to find herself caught up in the lives of the rural characters, and it was almost dawn before she laid the book aside and finally settled down to sleep.

Chapter Two

Carol was at her drawing board, putting the finishing touches on a drawing of a group of street kids break dancing, when the knock came at the door.

At first she didn't know whether to answer; she didn't know anyone in Rock Ridge and didn't yet feel at home in the area. She pulled back the yellow curtain she had hung on the window and looked out. A boy was standing in front of her door. He was a perfectly ordinary looking boy with jeans and running shoes and a navy windbreaker.

Still, perfectly ordinary boys sometimes committed extraordinary crimes, so even though she had grown up with brothers and was at ease with boys, instead of going to the door, she opened the window and called out hello.

The boy looked over at her, and she saw a face she instantly wanted to draw: tousled blond curly hair, dark blue eyes and features that came close to being classic except that his nose was a little off kilter, and so it was appealing instead.

"Ma'am?" he said.

"Yes, can I help you?"

He turned a smile on and off. "You the New York lady?"

"I'm Mr. Rafferty's tenant, yes."

The boy took a step back, then pointed up the road. "We're your closest neighbors, ma'am, up the road a ways. My dad asked me to stop by and see if you needed anything."

"What's your name?" asked Carol, wondering whether she ought to invite him inside.

"Willie, ma'am."

Carol closed the window and opened the door. "Come on in, Willie, but drop the ma'am, please. My name's Carol." Close up Carol saw how tall he was, at least five foot ten and probably still growing.

"Yes, ma'am," he said, entering the cabin and by sheer virtue of his height and the breadth of his shoulders, making it seem twice as small. Just as the "ma'ams" were making her feel twice her age.

She was about to motion him over to the kitchen table and offer him a Coke when his eyes lighted on her drawing and he moved closer in order to look at it.

"You draw this?" he asked, his accent every bit as thick as J. J. Rafferty's had been so that she found herself having to listen carefully to every word.

Carol made a noise of assent.

"That's real good, ma'am. There's a kid in my class draws almost as well as that. The teachers all say he's talented."

Not sure whether she was being flattered or denigrated, Carol kept silent.

"Could you draw me?"

"Probably."

He smiled again, and this time the smile lingered. "That's what you're going to do down here? Draw pictures? You an artist?"

"Commercial art," said Carol. "I do greeting cards, stuff like that."

"They pay you for it?"

"I support myself with it, yes."

He was looking impressed. "I never met a real artist before."

"Well, I'm not Picasso. I just do cards and calendars and things."

He was looking around the cabin now, and Carol wondered if he noticed the changes she had made. But all he said was, "You got any with you I could see?"

"No, I don't, but the stores around here probably carry them. Would you like a Coke?"

His attention quickly shifted. "Sure. Thanks, ma'am."

"Carol."

"Yeah. Carol."

She got out two Cokes and set them on the table, then took one of the chairs. She was lighting a cigarette as he sat down, and he said, "Could I have one? Please?"

She assessed his age as old enough that she didn't feel she was corrupting him and passed the pack over. He lit one smoothly, obviously practiced.

"I don't understand why your father asked you to stop by," she said.

"Old J.J. asked him to look in on you, see if you were doing okay, and Dad passed the job on to me."

"Your last name's Catlin?"

Willie nodded.

"Mr. Rafferty gave me his name to call in case I had any problems. I don't think I'll have any, though, but if I do—"

Willie looked disappointed. "Need any work done around here? I can cut firewood for you. You'll be needing a lot; it gets pretty cold here."

"Mr. Rafferty left me a big stack, but if I run out, I'll give you a call."

"That your car outside?"

Carol nodded.

"That's an awesome set of wheels. Nobody around here drives nothin' like that."

Warming to a subject dear to her heart, Carol said, "I've only had it a couple of months. Before that I hadn't had a car in years. I love it. It drove like a dream coming down here."

He grinned at her. "Don't suppose you need a chauffeur."

"Sorry, but I love driving."

"Yeah, me, too. I don't have my license yet, anyway, but I know how to drive. Need it washed or anything?"

Carol didn't mind the idea of washing it herself at all. She'd have the time, and she was still enthralled with the car, but it occurred to her that he might be desperate to make a little money, and she didn't want to begrudge him that.

"Okay, you got a deal," she told him. "A wash once a week and a wax job once a month. And if you know of anyone with a garage they'd rent me, I'd appreciate it. It'd have to be within walking distance, of course."

Willie's eyes widened. "Hey, you can use our garage. We don't park nothin' in it 'cause it's full of junk. I wouldn't mind cleaning it out for you."

"You better ask your dad first."

"He won't mind. He's been after me forever to clean it out."

"Ask him, anyway, and tell him I'd be willing to go twenty-five dollars a month on it."

He started to say something, then seemed to change his mind. And then, as though losing an argument with himself, he said, "That's too much. You don't want to go throwing away money like that."

Carol, who'd thrown away six times that much for garage space in New York, smiled. "Well, ask your dad and let me know. Anyway, he might not think it's too much."

He nodded, then downed his Coke in a few swallows. "How about rabbits? You interested in any?"

Visualizing bunnies in cages, Carol shook her head. "I really don't have room for them."

Willie glanced over at the refrigerator, then back to her. "I'll skin 'em for you and everything."

At the word "skin," Carol swallowed her Coke the wrong way and choked. When she could speak again, she said, "You mean rabbits to eat?"

"Sure, ma'am."

"No, I don't eat rabbits."

"Too bad, 'cause there's plenty of them around here. All you got to do is take old J.J's shotgun and walk a little ways in the woods. You wouldn't believe all the rabbits. Deer, too, but the hunting season on them hasn't started yet. I'll tell you what, ma'am. If you want, I'll do some hunting on J.J's property and split everything with you."

She wondered if he was bragging or whether they really allowed teenagers to have guns. "Unless my half is roast beef, forget it," she told him.

"You ever eaten venison?"

She shook her head.

"It's real good if you cook it right."

"Well, that leaves me out, then. My cooking runs more along the lines of frozen dinners."

The conversation winded down then, and she could tell he was trying to think of a polite way of leaving. Having had that trouble herself on more than one occasion, she helped him out. "If you don't mind, Willie, I have some work to do now. But let me know about the garage, okay? And any time you're ready to wash the car is fine."

He stood up and even carried his Coke can over to the sink, although she couldn't imagine that he expected her to wash out empty Coke cans. "Tomorrow's Saturday, I could do it for you in the morning."

For some reason she found herself loath to tell him that she was still sleeping until noon. Instead, she decided that this would force her to get up early and she could take that walk in the woods she had missed today. "Good, I'll see you then. And thanks for stopping by. Thank your dad for me, too."

She watched out the window after he left and smiled when he circled her car three times, more slowly each time. He even reached out a hand and carefully ran it over one of the fenders. Well, if he was that much in awe of it, he would no doubt do a good job of washing it for her.

"WHAT DO YOU THINK, Dad? I told her twenty-five was too much, but what I was figuring is, how about if we charge her thirty, and that includes keeping it clean and waxed."

Raney, who was more interested in eating his pork chops in peace than in hearing any more about the paragon with the Mercedes who was staying in J.J.'s cabin, scowled at his agitated son, the scowl intended to convey that he'd like a little quiet with his dinner.

The scowl failed. "She had this picture she drew, some black kids break dancing. You know what I mean? And anyway, she said she did that for a living. That she drew the pictures for stuff like birthday cards. You think she really does, or do you think she was putting me on?"

Raney swallowed the last of his pork chop, washed it down with some Bud and eyed his son. "Willie, will you unwind for a minute? To answer your first question, I don't care what you charge her to rent the garage. Just make sure that's where the car stays, okay? I don't want to be pulling up at night and have the driveway blocked; you understand me?" He waited for Willie's nod, then said, "How would I know what she does for a living? But someone's got to draw the pictures on those cards. Why not her? And it's something she could do at home, I guess; it's for sure she isn't going to find a job around here." Of course she could be rich, driving a Mercedes and all. But what would some rich New York lady want with J.J.'s cabin?

"She's nice, Dad, and real good-looking, too."

"You call that good-looking?"

Willie looked up from his food. "I thought you hadn't met her?"

Caught with having to give an embarrassing explanation, Raney improvised. "I happened to see her when I drove by yesterday. She didn't see me; I just caught a glimpse of her."

"Yeah, well take a second look. She's real pretty."

"Looked little and skinny to me."

"I'd say about five-four, maybe a hundred ten pounds."

Raney grinned. "You really looked her over, didn't you?"

"I have eyes. Pretty old; I'd say maybe twenty-five."

"I'd say closer to thirty."

"Cute figure; you know what I mean?"

Raney knew very well what he meant, but a cute figure was something a young girl had, not a grown woman. When you said a woman had a cute figure, it meant she was lacking. On the other hand, some of those high-school girls sure weren't lacking. "Yeah, well, be nice to her, Willie, but don't go overboard. The garage is okay—it'll be worth it to get it cleaned out. But don't be coming home next telling me you're renting her our spare room."

Willie was now looking even more agitated, and Raney couldn't figure out why. Then the kid said,

"Listen, Dad, I have a confession to make," and Raney felt indigestion coming on.

"I'm not sure I want to hear this."

"Look, I just don't want to do anything behind your back, okay? The truth of the matter is, I put a dent in the jeep—"

"You what?"

"Look, it was an accident, okay? The thing is, I'll be making some money now, and I just wanted you to know that I'll take care of it first thing. And I won't drive it again until I get my license, I swear."

Raney, who'd put more than one dent in his father's car when he was Willie's age, merely grunted. He made it a point never to confide in Willie about his own youth, because mischievous as Willie could sometimes be, he didn't come anywhere near being the hell raiser Raney had been, and he'd just as soon his son never found out about that.

"Hey, Dad, will you tell me something? Did old J.J. have curtains in that place? I haven't been inside it for a while, but I don't remember it looking the way it looked today."

"It didn't have curtains yesterday."

"It does now. Bright yellow. Also a yellow rug and a tablecloth and a bunch of pillows on the couch. It looked real nice—cheerful, you know?"

"Feminine."

"Maybe, I don't know. She was wearing yellow, too."

"Was she in a bathrobe?"

He could swear Willie was blushing. "Why would she be in a bathrobe? No, she was wearing jeans and a yellow sweater. I guess she likes yellow."

"I can't stand yellow."

"Her car's not yellow, anyway."

"Can we get serious for a minute and stop talking about the new neighbor? What're your plans tonight?"

"I don't know; just hanging out, I guess."

"I may stay out tonight, but I'll be calling here at midnight, and you better answer."

"Got a new girlfriend?"

Raney lifted one shoulder and let it drop. "Let's just say I'm working on it."

"Donna Lee, right?"

With a long-suffering sigh, Raney said, "If I wanted you to know the lady's name, I'd tell you, wouldn't I?"

"It's gotta be Donna Lee. Since her old man died—"

"His name was Glenn, and he was my friend, Willie."

"Movin' right in on her, huh?"

"If you're going to be smart, kid, you can stay home tonight."

"Sorry. I was just kidding around with you."

"You don't kid around about some things."

Willie's eyes grew round. "What do you mean? I hear you and your friends talking."

"Don't push me, okay? I did the cooking; now start cleaning up."

Raney went upstairs and took a look at himself in the bathroom mirror, trying to decide whether he ought to shave or not. Generally, he didn't ever bother shaving twice a day, but just on the off chance that Donna Lee was in the mood tonight, he figured it was worth the effort.

He'd always admired Donna Lee. She not only kept a good house for Glenn, but she never gave him a hard time as some of his friends' wives did. She kept herself nice, too, even after three kids. And no one would ever call Donna Lee's figure "cute." Awesome, maybe, to use one of Willie's current expressions, but never cute.

The parking lot to the Voyager Lounge was packed by the time Raney pulled in. He had to park blocking K.C.'s truck, but since K.C. generally closed the bar, it didn't worry him any. He checked out the cars, looking to see if Donna Lee was there yet, and finally spotted her Chevette.

The place didn't attract a young crowd. Those in their twenties headed for the other bar in town, the one that had pretentions of being a disco, with rock on the jukebox and a few flashing lights. Raney checked it out occasionally, but it always made him feel old. The people didn't even dress the same there. Instead of boots, a lot of the younger men were wearing running shoes these days. Not that any of them did any real running, but he figured they thought they were rock stars or something.

He saw Donna Lee at the end of the bar as he walked in, and after greeting a few people and picking up a beer and a shot of bourbon from Marcie, who tended bar on the weekends, he headed down in her direction.

"How's it going?" he asked her, taking out his lighter when he saw her pulling out a cigarette. She was looking real good in pants and a matching jacket in a nice shade of blue and some kind of silky-looking blouse underneath with ruffles. But then Donna Lee had always been a sharp dresser.

"Pretty good, Raney." She leaned over for the light, and he got a quick glimpse of what lay beneath the blouse.

He heard a slow tune coming up on the jukebox but figured it was too soon to make his move. Instead, he bought Donna Lee a drink and began to stake out his territory. Which was going to be necessary, as the rest of the women in there were married, with the exception of the bartender, and she had a long-standing boyfriend. With a quick count, he came up with five other men who could possibly be after Donna Lee. Three were unmarried, and the other two were married but ran around. Which wasn't easy in Rock Ridge. First of all, there weren't enough women running around to supply the men who ran around, and second of all, the place was so damn small it was hard to get away with anything.

He made some small talk with Donna Lee, threw a few compliments her way, which always went over big with the ladies, and when the third slow dance came up, he nodded toward the dance floor and said, "Want to try it?"

Shrugging to show she didn't care either way and also conveying to him that she wasn't a pushover,

Donna Lee followed him out on the floor. He put his arms around her waist, and she put hers around his neck; then he moved to within an inch of her body and bided his time. When he finally made his move, though, about halfway through the song, Donna Lee didn't keep her voice low when she said, "Move the hands right back up, Raney Catlin," which got a laugh from some of the people at the bar.

"Sorry about that, Donna Lee."

"Don't give me that sorry stuff, Raney. You used to try the same thing on me in high school, if you recall."

He recalled, all right, but he thought she was a little more experienced these days. Hell, he knew she was more experienced. She had three kids, didn't she?

Then, purely by habit, he moved his elbows in close to her breasts, getting a feel in the process. This time, though, Donna Lee drew back from him, muttered a few choice words and stalked back to the bar. At that point, Raney figured the shave had been a waste of time.

Acting contrite, Raney went back to the bar and said, "Sorry if I acted out of turn, Donna Lee. You're a good-looking woman, you know—"

"We're not in high school anymore, Raney, and I know all your tricks. Furthermore, you think you're the first man who tried to move in on me since Glenn passed away?"

By that time he had a pretty good idea he was going to beat Willie home. "I apologize again, Donna Lee. I just figured maybe you were as lonely as I am."

Donna Lee gave a snort of laughter. "Yeah, Raney, I heard how lonely you've been."

Raney turned an innocent face in her direction.

"And don't give me that innocent look, either. You think everyone in town don't know when you visit Maybelle?"

At least Maybelle didn't give him any back talk. It was a business proposition, pure and simple. And most of the time Raney figured he'd rather rent his women than own them. What'd Donna Lee think she was, some prize with three school-age kids? Except in their town she probably was.

"Hey, Donna Lee, remember that dance we went to in high school? The night Bubba Hollis spiked the punch?"

"Can't say that I do, Raney."

"Sure you do. You had three cups before you caught on to it, and we went out to the parking lot?"

"We're not in high school anymore, Raney."

Which was the truth, but sometimes Raney wished they were. It had been good in those days. He'd been on the football team; the girls all admired him. Well, maybe not all the girls. Now that he recalled correctly, Donna Lee had never exactly been easy. Like most of the girls, she had been holding out for marriage. And what was really funny when he thought about it, the ones that held out and the ones that didn't hold out all ended up the same. Married with kids. Except Maybelle, of course, but then all the boys had known that Maybelle was particularly talented.

If he was in high school now, he'd tell Donna Lee just where to go; only he wasn't and she was the only game in town at the moment. And then he felt really guilty even thinking that, because he'd been Glenn's friend and he should be acting nicer to the widow, not giving her a hard time.

Remorseful, he turned to her and put his hand on her shoulder. "Hey, Donna Lee, I really do apologize. You and Glenn were like family to me, and if there's ever anything you need, all you have to do is ask."

Donna Lee leaned over and gave him a quick kiss on the cheek. "I know, Raney, and I appreciate it. I'm not all that over Glenn yet, you know?"

Well, there was nothing to say to that, so he just nodded. And then the door to the Voyager opened, and the person who walked in just about stopped all conversation dead.

Raney's first thought was that someone got the two bars in town mixed up; then he took a better look and saw that it was the New York lady from J.J.'s cabin. Only she was wearing the weirdest getup the occupants of the Voyager had ever seen.

If Raney had to describe it to someone, the closest he could get to an apt description would have been that she looked as if she were in army fatigues; only they weren't like any army fatigues he had ever seen. And instead of boots or high heels on her feet, she was wearing sneakers patterned like camouflage. But even in a regular getup she would have looked different, because her hair wasn't long and straight or short and puffed out; it was just medium length and kind of hanging around her face, natural like. And like the glimpse of her he had gotten the night before, she still wasn't wearing a particle of makeup. What it was, she was dressed like some kid, not like a woman ought to dress at all.

Every pair of eyes at the bar were turned in her direction, and he saw that she looked like a scared rabbit cornered by a dog. He just about took pity on her and maybe would have gone to her rescue, but Donna Lee said to him, "Who the hell is that?" And he turned to her and started to explain about J.J.'s letting his cabin, and when he got around to turning back, the woman had vanished.

But hell, she should've known better than to walk into the Voyager Lounge. Any stranger would've got the same treatment.

CAROL HAD NEVER FELT so stupid in her entire life.

She had seen the Voyager Lounge on her way shopping, had surmised it was a neighborhood hangout, the kind of place where the local people would congregate at night to have a few drinks and be sociable. She figured Rock Ridge wasn't New York, that it would be a perfectly respectable thing to do, just to drop in, introduce herself, get to meet some of her neighbors. She was sure it wouldn't be a singles bar, the kind of place she avoided in New York. Nor would she likely be hit upon or hustled in any way. And small towns were friendly places, weren't they? Didn't small-town people generally welcome strangers, make them feel at home?

Still, all this generalizing notwithstanding, it had taken a certain amount of courage on her part to psych herself up to where she could walk into a strange bar all alone. Never mind feeling comfortable once she got in there. She hadn't expected to feel comfortable immediately, but she was hoping to get to know a few people and have a place where she could go at night to relax when she needed more than a book for company.

She told herself as she approached the door to the lounge that she'd act casual, smile at the people, order herself a beer and just sit down and relax for a few minutes and see what happened. Well, what actually happened was that she was made to feel like an alien from outer space. Just her appearance in the doorway had caused all conversation to stop, all eyes to turn in her direction, and if she was reading those eyes correctly—and she was certain she was—all she could read in them was hostility.

In the split second it took for her to gauge the atmosphere, she swore she would not panic and run, and then she did exactly that. And on the short drive home she berated herself for chickening out, for not even putting herself out a little to be friendly. She was the newcomer, after all. She could have made the effort.

But she could never remember feeling as relieved as she felt when she was once more in her cabin, away from prying eyes.

So she wasn't the bar type. Okay, she'd always known that. Even parties where she didn't know anyone were difficult for her. And it wasn't shyness, either; at least she didn't think so. On a one-to-one basis she could talk to anyone. On airplane flights she often initiated conversations. When she took an occasional night class, she would be the one to pull the group together, to suggest they go out after class.

Well, she had always known she was bad at bar scenes. One of the more humiliating moments of her life had been when her agent had asked to meet her one evening in a bar near the agent's office. Being the type who was always on time, if not early, Carol had gotten there a few minutes early. Knowing she was going to meet someone, though, made her less uneasy about sitting at a bar all alone.

But when her agent was delayed and the few minutes turned into a half hour and Carol looked around her and saw there was only one other woman there and she was with someone, she began to imagine that every man in the bar thought she was there with the express purpose of being picked up. She had panicked and left and then had been laughed at later by her agent, a woman who had no problems walking into any bar in the city and feeling right at home.

She told herself to forget about it. She had come to Rock Ridge for quiet, for solitude. And she had found it, too. She didn't need to go to the local bar. She didn't even need to meet people. She was self-sufficient and able to amuse herself.

It would just take a little while to get used to after living in the city, that's all. She wasn't accustomed to being unable to just lift up the phone and call a friend or even turn on the TV if she wanted the sound of voices. She would adjust, just as she had learned to adjust to the city.

But first thing in the morning she was going to get herself a TV set.

Chapter Three

Raney was just pulling up in his pickup truck when Carol came out of his garage. He saw her glance at the truck, then turn around and pull down the door.

He got out of the truck, then leaned back against the door and figured he better introduce himself, if for no other reason than his kid talked about nothing else these days. He'd heard the name Carol so many times at the dinner table he would've figured that Willie had a new girlfriend if he didn't know better.

"I guess I ought to meet Willie's friend," he said to her, making a joke of it. "I'm Raney Catlin."

She walked up to him and held out her hand. "Carol Jones. How're you doing?"

He wasn't used to shaking hands with ladies, but what the hell. He figured it was going to be some kind of limp shake, but she grasped his hand firmly and gave one quick shake, then let loose of it and hooked her thumbs in the pockets of her jeans. She reminded him of a boy, the way she acted—the handshake, hooking the thumbs, the way she looked him straight in the eye. No flirting, none of that, just straightforward.

He tried to think of something else to say and finally came up with, "Garage working out okay?" That would give her an opening, he figured.

"Fine."

Didn't talk much for a woman, either. "Willie's not making a pest of himself, is he? Kid's got a tendency to do that."

But she just said, "I like Willie," which could mean he was or he wasn't making a pest of himself, but obviously she didn't mind if he was.

She looked better up close. She didn't have the kind of features that stood out at a distance, particularly with no kind of makeup on, but her eyes were a real dark brown with thick lashes and straight dark brows, and her hair was a lighter shade of brown and looked clean and silky, as if she'd just washed it. She seemed to be all straight lines—her nose, her mouth, her long, slim legs in the skinny jeans.

"Nice meeting you," she said, and started to walk past him, and he wanted to keep her there for a minute, to get to know her a little. He felt he ought to check out Willie's friends, after all.

"Why'd you walk out of the bar so fast?" he asked, wanting to shock her a little and get some reaction out of her.

She turned back to him and avoided his eyes this time. "You were there?"

"Sure was."

"I must've looked pretty stupid."

He thought of the way she had been dressed and felt like agreeing, but then he realized she probably wasn't referring to her clothes. He was sure she wouldn't choose to dress that way if she thought it made her look stupid. "You looked like a scairt rabbit to me."

She gave a quick smile that brought out a couple of dimples and made her look so alive he found himself wanting to make her smile again. "I guess I felt like a scared rabbit. I've never been very good at walking into bars, but that's the first time I've stopped all the conversation with my appearance."

"It's just that everyone'd been wondering about you."

"What're you talking about?"

"Soon as you hit town and asked Bubba for directions, that's all it took. A stranger around here is news."

"I've never lived in a small town."

"Hell, this isn't even a small town. This is country, honey."

He saw the wary look come into her eyes then but didn't know the reason. She was looking down at her feet when she said, "Well, it won't happen again."

"You mean walking into the bar?"

She nodded.

He found himself saying, "Hey, any night you want to go to the Voyager, just let me know. I'll introduce you around. Everyone's real friendly when you get to know them." Even as he said it, he wondered why he was offering. Well, some of the guys might go for her, if for no other reason than she'd be a novelty.

She said, "Thanks, I appreciate the offer. I might take you up on it one of these days."

"How about tonight?"

There was a silence; then she said, "I've got to finish up some work tonight so I can mail it out tomorrow. But thanks."

"How about tomorrow night?"

Her eyes seemed to widen at his persistence, and he was just as surprised himself, particularly since tomorrow night was Friday and he usually tried to find himself a woman on Friday nights. Not that he'd been succeeding all that much lately.

She seemed to be hesitating, so he said, "Come on, you'll meet all your neighbors."

"All right." But she sure didn't sound thrilled about it.

"Good, I'll swing around by your place about eight. That suit you?"

She didn't say anything, just nodded; then she turned and headed down the road toward her cabin. Not a goodbye, nothing. She sure didn't appear to like wasting words.

"Met your friend Carol," he said to Willie later on that evening when they were eating dinner.

"Yeah? What'd you think of her?"

"Doesn't say much."

Willie looked surprised. "She talks to me all the time."

"I offered to take her down to the Voyager, introduce her around."

"You're taking her out?" He sounded accusing.

"No, I'm not taking her out. I just offered to introduce her to her neighbors, that's all."

"I don't think she's your type, Dad."

"I know damn well she's not my type. It just seemed the right thing to do. She walked in there one night and walked right back out."

"You never told me that."

"Forgot about it."

"She's nice, Dad, and I don't think she's had much experience."

"How would you know about that?"

"Well, I know she's never been married."

"What's that got to do with having experience?"

"It's just my opinion, that's all."

"Well, let me educate you a little, Willie. You don't live in a place like New York and not get experience."

IF SHE HAD A TELEPHONE, she would have called Raney Catlin and tried to get out of it. Not that she was worried he was thinking of it as a date any more than she was, but Carol hadn't liked him, and she didn't look forward to spending an evening in his company.

She hadn't liked the way he had looked at her, assessing her, and she hadn't liked the way he'd called her honey. He looked okay, like an older, more worn version of his son, but she didn't go by looks when it came to her own assessment of men. Mostly she went by intelligence and attitude, and he didn't strike her as particularly intelligent, and he seemed to have the kind of macho attitude she hated in a man. In fact, she had heard of rednecks, and she was pretty sure Raney

Catlin was one. And she'd never heard the word used in any kind of complimentary context.

One thing was for sure: she wasn't going to worry about how she was dressed this time. She'd just wear her jeans and Nikes and a navy blue cashmere V-neck men's sweater she felt comfortable in. She hadn't got a good enough look at the people in the bar to remember how they were dressed, but from her drives around the area it appeared that just about everyone under forty wore jeans all the time.

She was ready to go twenty minutes before Raney was due to pick her up and smoked six ciagrettes in quick succession while she waited for him. No matter what she called it, it was beginning to feel like a date, and she hated the feeling.

She tried to convince herself that Raney Catlin probably wasn't that bad, that his son was okay and it was possible he took after his father, but she really wasn't convinced. Anyway, most kids she knew weren't anything like their parents.

Willie never mentioned his mother, which made Carol wonder about her. She figured she probably was dead, or else Willie would be living with her. Maybe Raney would mention her, but she wouldn't ask him outright. It wasn't any of her business, and she didn't want to pry. And yet she was no doubt the only person in the entire county who didn't have the answer to that question.

At ten minutes after eight she figured he forgot about it and felt a great sense of relief. She was just about to get into her robe and watch some TV when she heard the truck pull up and then, a moment later, the sound of a door slamming, and she felt exactly the same way she always felt on her arrival at her dentist's office. Which wasn't exactly a great feeling.

RANEY FIGURED that being a lady, she'd keep him waiting, but he hadn't even got to her door before it opened and she was outside. He took one look at her and said, "Better wear a coat or something; it's supposed to go down to forty tonight."

He saw her nod, then go back inside, and he walked over to the cabin door and looked inside. Yeah, Willie had been right. Lots of yellow stuff around, and it looked pretty nice. Big color TV set, too. Old J.J. wouldn't recognize it if he returned unexpectedly.

She was grabbing something out of the closet and putting it on, and he saw it was a leather jacket, but real old and worn looking, the kind most people threw away. It also had real large padded shoulders that looked pretty funny on such a small woman.

She walked ahead of him out to the truck and had the door handle in her hand before he could open it for her. Well, that was okay with him. If she wanted to act like one of the boys, let her. He'd save his energy for the real ladies.

He could tell by the way she lit a cigarette, once they were on the road, that she was tense, and he said, "Relax; no one's going to bite you."

"I just feel stupid after having walked right back out the other night. Some of the same people might be there."

Raney chuckled. "All of the same people will be there. Listen, you're something of a celebrity around here; the folks are all dying to meet you."

"A celebrity for what?"

"Those cards you draw. Willie told me about them, and the card store over in Bradford carries them. Everyone's been going over and taking a look at them."

She glanced over at him and grinned. "Did you run over there to look at them?"

"I didn't have to; Willie must've bought out the store. He has them hanging all over his room."

"He didn't have to do that; I would've got him some."

He said, "They're kind of cute," then could tell by her silence that his compliment hadn't gone over all that well. But what else would you call drawings of kids if not cute? And it's not as if she were Norman Rockwell or something. "Would you rather be drawing something else?"

"No."

Well, that ended that line of conversation. "What made you want to move down here?" he asked, wanting to get her talking, relax her.

"I was getting tired of New York."

"So you just decided to take off?"

"I can work anywhere. I felt like some quiet."

"Well, we got plenty of that."

He was saved from having to come up with another conversational gambit by reaching the Voyager. He found a parking space, and by the time he got around to her side of the truck, she was already out and had locked the door.

"You don't have to lock it up around here."

He saw a flash of dimples; then she said, "I keep forgetting. In New York you have to lock everything up."

"We get our share of things being stolen, I expect, but there's nothing in my truck worth stealing."

She appeared to be rooted to the spot in the parking lot, so he took her hand and pulled it through his arm and said, "Come on; if you survive the first five minutes, you'll be okay."

"It's the first five minutes I'm worried about," she said, but she sounded more relaxed, and he thought it was going to be okay. And he kind of liked the idea that he was the one bringing the celebrity into the bar. Maybe Donna Lee would get jealous and pay more attention to him. Yeah, and maybe fleas would stay off dogs, too.

CAROL HAD NEVER WANTED to be an actress or a singer or anyone else who had to get up in front of the public and get all that attention. But that's exactly the way she felt when she walked into the Voyager with Raney.

It wasn't quite as bad as walking in by herself, though, and everyone immediately called out to Raney, which diverted some of the attention from her, but she could tell that even though the words were for him, they were all pretty much sizing her up.

He took her completely around the bar, introducing her to everyone, and she shook more hands and

heard more names than she would ever be able to remember. She also took in the way the women were
dressed: the thin ones wore jeans and shirts and cow-
boy boots, and the ones who were more spread out in
the hips wore polyester pantsuits with either heels or
boots. Not that she was about to go out and buy similar clothes, but she didn't think she looked too out of
place, anyway.

There was an empty bar stool next to a woman
named Donna Lee, and Raney motioned for her to sit
down. Donna Lee had a sweet face and an abundance
of blond hair and the most godawful electric-blue
pantsuit Carol had ever seen. With her artist's eye she
was already washing off Donna Lee's makeup, shap-
ing her hair and redressing her, but then she realized
how pretentious it was of her and forced herself to
knock it off. Anyway, despite the woman's makeup
and hair and clothes, she appeared to be the belle of
the ball and had a cluster of men around her vying to
buy her drinks.

"What're you having?" Raney asked her, and when
she said whatever beer was on draft, he looked a little
surprised. He probably figured she was going to order a Manhattan or a martini or something, but beer
was about the only thing she ever drank.

When the glass of beer was set in front of her, Carol
reached in her pocket and pulled out a twenty, then set
it on the bar.

"Put your money away," said Raney, and she didn't
like the way he said it.

"I'll pay for my own," she told him.

"Not when you're with me, you won't."

She could hear the conversation around them come to a halt, and Donna Lee was listening to the exchange with interest.

"In fact," Carol said, "I'd like to buy you a drink. After all, you gave me a ride over here." She did want to buy him a drink, but she also wanted everyone to know that she wasn't there with Raney, at least in any other sense than that they rode there together.

"You northerners all this stubborn?" Raney asked her, and he had his eyes narrowed in a way that made him look a little scary.

"Hey, Raney, you can buy me a drink," said Donna Lee.

Several of the other people around said, "Yeah, me, too, Raney," and then there was some laughter, and she saw Raney relax a little.

Donna Lee nudged her and said in a low voice, "Let him pay, girl. Raney can afford it."

"So can I," said Carol, but she lightened the words with a smile.

"In other words," said Donna Lee, "you don't want to feel obligated to Raney. Can't say that I blame you there." She said it loudly enough for Raney to hear.

"Bad-mouthing me again?" Raney asked her.

"Just setting her straight," said Donna Lee, smiling. "Don't want the town celebrity to get off on the wrong foot."

Raney was grinning now. "And I'm the wrong foot?"

"If the shoe fits, Raney..."

Some of the men around Raney started to talk about the Georgia Tech game the next day, discussing point spreads, holes in the defense, just regular football talk, and Carol was listening, preferring that kind of talk to small talk or women talk, which she was never very good at. Then, just as it was turning into a heated debate and really getting interesting, she saw Raney watching her, and then he was asking her if she wanted to dance.

"No, thanks."

"Smart lady," murmured Donna Lee.

"Well, see if I ask you to dance after that remark," Raney said.

"Don't do me no favors, Raney."

The music was some lively country tune, and Carol watched the dancers for a minute, but she couldn't tell what they were doing. It wasn't any kind of dance she had ever seen.

"You don't like to dance?" Raney asked her.

"Not really."

"I thought all women liked to dance."

"What he means," said Donna Lee, "is that he thought all women liked to dance with him."

"The hell with you," Raney told Donna Lee, then went back to talking with the men.

"Watch out for him when he's had a few too many," Donna Lee advised her.

"Watch out for what?"

"Oh, I don't mean he'd try nothing with you; it's just that Raney has a way of getting into fights. Not that he's alone, mind you; a lot of the guys are that way. Just don't say nothing to him when he's in that mood that he might take wrong.''

Carol really didn't want any advice regarding Raney, as she didn't plan on being around him enough to need it. She figured if she got through this one evening, he would have felt he had done his duty and never ask her again. And if he did ask her again, she'd say she did her work at night.

She wouldn't mind having a friend, though; someone to occasionally go to a movie with or out to eat. And she didn't think making a friend in the area was going to be all that easy. But Donna Lee appeared to be single, and she was certainly friendly, so she said, ''What do you do, Donna Lee?''

''Do?''

''Don't you work?''

''I got three kids to take care of, and if you don't think that's work—''

''Sorry, I didn't know you were married.'' But now that she was looking, she saw the wedding ring on the woman's finger.

''He died, about eight months ago. Raney was one of his best friends.''

''I'm sorry. That must be rough with three kids.''

''It isn't the kids that make it rough; I'd go nuts if I didn't have them. It's Glenn I miss—just having a man around. You know what I mean?''

''Not really,'' said Carol. She had never had a man around long enough to miss him, and she couldn't remember her mother ever missing her father.

''You never been married?'' she asked, making it sound as if Carol were some kind of freak.

"I'm only thirty," said Carol.

"Only thirty? Girl, I'm only thirty-four, and I've been married sixteen years. Don't you want children?"

"Did you?"

Donna Lee burst out laughing, a rich, hearty sound that made Carol smile. "If you mean did I plan them, no. And after the third I told Glenn he better use something or else find him someone on the side."

Carol was taken aback at the confidence; she would never have confided in a stranger that way. At least not about something as intimate as birth control. "Raney's son's a good kid," she said, just to change the subject.

"Yeah, Raney keeps him in line. Got the kid real intimidated. Willie should only know what a devil his daddy was at that age. Girl, I could tell you stories..."

Carol nodded. "I had some brothers like that."

"Yeah, you know boys, then. Willie tell you about his mother?"

"No, not a word. I assumed she died."

"Charlene? Raney probably wishes she'd died." She looked around as though to see if Raney was in hearing distance, then lowered her voice and said, "Charlene got strange."

"Strange?"

"I'd say religious, except I don't consider that strange. Most of us around here are Baptists and go to church on Sunday, but Charlene—well, I don't rightly know how to put it. She started taking the Bible literal, you know? She changed so I hardly recognized her no more, and we used to be real close."

Carol was still left wondering what happened to Charlene, but she didn't want to ask. Instead, she said, "I guess all of you grew up together."

"Oh, sure—everyone knows everyone else's business. And of course everyone wants to hear about you. I'll be the star of the beauty shop tomorrow when I tell them I talked to you."

"Make me more interesting," said Carol. "Tell them I've been married six times."

"That wouldn't make you interesting around here. Never even been married once is far more interesting. And being from New York is the icing on the cake. Bet you have a real time of it up there."

"That depends on what you mean by a real time of it."

"I mean men. What else?"

Carol chuckled. "I'm not all that big on men, but even if I were, good men aren't that easy to find in New York."

"Good men aren't that easy to find anywhere. You're a cute little thing, though, and if you take a look around the bar, I'll bet you'll find half the men have their eyes on you already."

Carol raised her brows at the "cute little thing" but didn't say anything. "I didn't come here to meet men," she said, wanting to set that straight.

"I could tell that straight away. You wouldn't be wasting your time talking to me all night if you were looking for a man.

"I don't consider it a waste of time."

"Will you tell me something, Carol?"

"Sure."

"Why'd you walk out so fast the other night?"

"I'm just not very good at walking into strange bars by myself."

Donna Lee was nodding. "Yeah, I figured it was something like that. Now take me, I know everyone here, so it's just like my home. But you wouldn't catch me going to Atlanta and walking into some lounge. Not all by myself, anyway. Tell you what, honey; I'm in here every Friday and Saturday night. I'll save you a seat, and if you want to come in and shoot the bull with me, just don't you hesitate. And I won't let none of the men bother you, either."

"I appreciate that. Being in that cabin alone all the time without even a phone, I'm starting to talk to myself."

"You got to come over to dinner some night, meet my kids. Not that that's any great privilege I'm bestowing on you."

"I like kids."

"Yeah?"

"Sometimes I think I like them better than adults."

"What do you like better than adults?" Raney was back.

"Kids," volunteered Donna Lee.

"Yeah, I knew that already. She's got Willie in a daze. Course it isn't all that difficult to get Willie in a daze."

"I like Willie," said Carol.

"Yeah, well he likes you, too. In fact, I think he more than likes you."

Carol said, "We're friends."

Raney grinned. "I'm sure that's true on your part, but my son has a pretty big crush on you."

"I thought he was going with Linda," said Donna Lee.

"She calls him up all the time, but Willie don't seem that interested in her anymore."

Carol had heard all about Linda from Willie but wasn't about to reveal the boy's confidences. Nor did she take the crush seriously. Willie needed someone to talk to, that was all, and she didn't mind listening or even giving advice if it was asked for.

Carol had noticed the men going in and out of a back room all night, and to get off the subject of Willie, she asked Raney what was back there.

"Couple of pool tables."

"Are the women allowed back there?"

Donna Lee chuckled. "We got our rights down here, same as up in New York."

"Want to shoot a game?"

Donna Lee looked surprised. "Me? I never even played with Glenn, and he had a pool table in the basement. Course most of the time it was piled with laundry.

"You know how to play?" Raney was asking her.

"I used to play with my brothers when I was a kid."

"I'll play a game with you." He looked really amused, as if he were humoring her. Or maybe hustling her.

Donna Lee said, "Watch out for Raney or he'll take all your money."

"Is that right?" Carol asked him.

Raney shrugged. "Maybe, but I'm still willing to buy your drinks."

RANEY COULDN'T WAIT to walk into the back room with Carol. Whether women were allowed in there or not, it was the men's province, and most of them wanted to keep it that way. He'd get hell from them later, but he'd tell them he didn't have any choice, that the New York lady had wanted to shoot pool and he was just obliging her. And he was sure that after one game she would never want to visit the back room again.

Oh, he had no doubt that she could shoot a little pool. If she grew up shooting pool with her brothers, she had probably learned something along the way. She shouldn't be a total embarrassment to him. But she wasn't in his league; half the men in the county weren't in his league when it came to shooting pool.

Anyway, she needed some paying back for making such a fuss about his buying her beer. He hadn't liked that. First woman he had ever met who wouldn't accept a free drink. And wanting to buy him a drink? Forget it. The day Raney Catlin let a gal buy his drinks for him—well, that'd be a sorry day for sure. He figured they got things backward in New York City: the men must be acting like women and the women like men, or else how did you account for it?

Well, this was Rock Ridge, not New York City, and the little lady had a lot to learn. And if he had the time or the inclination, he'd teach her. As it was, she'd just have to learn all by herself.

The silence was absolute when the guys saw him walking into the back room with Carol. He glanced down at her, but unlike the night she walked into the bar alone, this didn't seem to unnerve her. Her eyes scanned the two tables, then went to Raney.

"What do we have to do, challenge them?"

"In this particular case," said Raney, "I think they'll give up one of the tables. Right, guys? The lady and I want to shoot a little pool."

Wayne looked over at him and rolled his eyes. "Just give me one more minute at the table, Raney, and it's all yours."

Carol walked over to the wall rack and lifted down a few cue sticks, one at a time, until she found one she held on to. Raney figured she must have seen her brothers do that and copied them. Trying to be like one of the boys. Well, if she wanted to be one of the boys, he was sure going to give her the opportunity. Just too bad she was set on making such a damn fool of herself. Her mama should have brought her up to behave like a lady.

When the table was open, Raney put in two quarters and racked the balls. Then, thinking he'd give the room a good laugh, he asked her if she wanted to break.

She didn't say a word, just nodded briefly and positioned herself for the break. A couple of guys whistled low when the break was good, scattering the balls and sinking two low ones in what Raney considered a pure stroke of luck. He waited for her to turn to him and smile, maybe say it was a lucky shot or something, try to get his approval, but she didn't even look up from the table. And in quick succession she sunk two more, then, on the next shot, she did glance up and see him, and for some reason, that seemed to fluster her, because she missed a real easy shot that even a girl should've got.

She moved away from the table, and one of the guys yelled out, "Hey, Raney, looks like she missed that one on purpose just to give you a break," and for a moment Raney nearly saw red. He couldn't think of anything more humiliating than a woman letting him beat her at pool.

But Carol answered him right back, saying, "You don't know me if you think that," and for some reason he believed her.

Five minutes later Raney was wishing he'd stayed home that night. When she beat him in nothing flat, it wasn't the guys' razzing that got to him so much as the cool way Carol handled herself. She didn't scream with joy or even look triumphant. No, it was much worse than that. She acted as if it were only natural she won, and she was already reaching into her pocket and then putting two quarters into the slots before he could tell her he'd had enough.

Except he really couldn't say that, not with all the guys around. It would make him look like a poor sport, as if he minded being beaten by a woman. Even though everyone in the room, with the possible exception of Carol, knew for a fact that was true.

It galled him to have to admit it, but he admired her style at the table. She used precise, economical movements, didn't do any grandstanding, and what's more, she called every shot accurately. In fact, she stroked them almost exactly the way he played, except he had to admit he grandstanded on occasion.

He won the next two games, but not by much, and he figured she'd want to quit then, but she just said, "Three out of five?" and of course he had to agree to it. Which wasn't his smartest move of the night, because she won the next two handily.

At the finish of the fifth game, she calmly put back her cue, then turned to him and said, "You can buy me that drink now." And then all the guys in the room gave her a cheer, and she nodded her head in their direction before heading back to the bar.

Raney was glad to see that Donna Lee was dancing, because he didn't feel like hearing any replay of their games. Then he remembered that he was after Donna Lee himself and checked out whom she was dancing with. But somehow he didn't even care that it was Daryl, because he found that he really wasn't in the mood for women that night. Even if Donna Lee up and offered herself to him, he would probably turn her down. Well, maybe he wouldn't go that far...

They took two seats at the bar, and some of the guys from the back room came out, and Raney could tell they were telling everybody what happened. Then a couple of them came over and introduced themselves to Carol and told her they'd never seen a woman who shot such good pool. She didn't act coy or anything or say she wasn't all that good—which was a good thing, since she had beaten him. She just thanked them and ordered a beer for herself and some bourbon for Raney, then sat there and minded her own business.

"Your brothers taught you to shoot pool, huh?" Raney asked her.

"No, my father taught all of us."

Raney digested that for a moment, "What else did he teach you?"

Her smile briefly flashed; then she said, kind of kidding, "All kinds of things, really."

He grinned at her, hoping to see an answering smile, but he was disappointed. "Didn't he teach you how to drink bourbon?"

This time she did smile and hold it, making him wish she smiled more often. "He probably would have if he'd stuck around that long. Last time I saw him I was twelve, though, and I guess he figured that was too young."

Raney felt sorry for any twelve-year-old whose father took off, and with only sympathy in mind, he put his hand on her shoulder and squeezed. The smile disappeared in an instant, and he knew he had made the wrong move. He took his hand off, offered her a smoke, then said, "You got me curious now; I'm wondering what else he taught you."

"You play poker?"

"Forget it, lady. We might allow women in the pool room, but we sure as hell don't allow them in our poker games."

She shrugged. "You wanted to know what he taught me. Anyway, I haven't played poker in years. Not since—"

"You played with your brothers," he finished for her, and she nodded. "Were you one of those tomboys?"

"I never really had a choice."

He didn't know about that. He and his brother had a younger sister, and she had never been a tomboy. But then he didn't know all that much about her family circumstances.

She said, "Would you mind if I went home now? I'd be glad to call a taxi if you don't want to leave."

"No problem," he told her. "I can always come back." That is, if he felt like getting kidded the rest of the night about losing at pool to a lady.

"Thanks."

She sure was economical with words. He watched as she walked down the bar to say good-night to Donna Lee; then he went out to the truck with her. This time he beat her to the door, but then he had to unlock it for her, anyway. She didn't thank him or anything, just got in and reached over and opened his door for him. In other words, getting the last word, so to speak.

They rode in silence until they got to her cabin. Then all she said was "Thanks, I enjoyed it," and before he could even suggest they do it again, she was out of the truck and headed for her door.

Which was just as well, because he had no intention of asking her to do it again. But he couldn't help wondering if she could beat him at poker.

He didn't really reckon she could. Hell, lightning didn't strike the same place twice, did it?

WILLIE REALLY HATED the fact that his father was out with Carol. Not that he didn't like it when his father had a girlfriend; his dad was much more mellow at those times and even cut down on the drinking.

But he just couldn't see his dad and Carol. Carol wasn't anything like the women Raney usually went for. And he was pretty sure Carol didn't like men like his dad, either. He figured she went for artistic types, men who had something in common with her, who could carry on intelligent conversations.

Someone like him, only a little older, of course.

He was aware that his feelings for Carol were verging on the kind of feelings he got for girls he had gone with at school, but there was a big difference. He could really talk to Carol. He could tell her just about anything, and she would listen, and she never criticized him.

He knew that if his friends knew about her they would figure he was using her as some substitute mother, but that was about as far from the truth as you could get. A sister would be closer, but he really didn't feel brotherly toward her. If it was brotherly feelings he was having, he was sure they wouldn't be keeping him awake nights.

The main reason his friends didn't know about her was that he was spending most of his free time with Carol. The thing was, she was a lot more fun and a lot more interesting than his friends. Anyway, he saw enough of his friends at school and at football practice. After that, he felt like hanging around Carol and just talking about things.

She never seemed bored with him, either. He watched out for that—watched out to see if he was boring people. Because personally he couldn't stand being around boring people. But she always seemed interested in what he had to say, and she always invited him in with a smile and gave him a Coke. And when she had work to do, she would tell him, and he would leave, but there were never any hard feelings about it.

She was a lot different from any of the girls he had gone with. For one thing, she didn't giggle all the time. In fact, she didn't giggle at all. And she didn't try to act cute or like a little girl, the way some of the mothers of the girls he knew acted, and all of the girls. She just acted like a regular person. And she treated him like an adult, too.

He had given it a great deal of thought, and he didn't think he was too young for her. If she would only hold off and not get married in the next three years, he would be eighteen and could do anything he wanted. And if she wanted to get married, he'd be willing. And that was saying a lot, because before he met her, he planned on staying single for his whole life.

The hardest part about being around her so much was that he wanted to touch her. Not make moves on her, nothing like that, but just maybe reach out and touch her arm when they were talking or even give her a hug or something. Nothing else. He didn't even let himself think about anything else.

But Carol wasn't a toucher. Most of the people he knew were, but Carol never even got that close. He guessed maybe that was because she was from New

York. Maybe in New York it was dangerous to go around touching people.

What he really felt like doing at the moment was sneaking out of the house, taking the jeep and driving down to the Voyager to spy on his father and Carol. He just hoped his father wouldn't do anything or say anything that would make Carol not be his friend anymore. It was just that you could never tell what Raney was going to do.

When he finally heard his father come home, he was surprised not to hear the door slam or the familiar cursing or any other indication that Raney'd had too much to drink.

When his dad walked past his bedroom door, Willie called out, "How'd it go?"

There was silence for a moment; then Raney walked in and turned on the overhead light. "You might as well hear it from me, as it'll be all over town tomorrow."

Willie hoped it wasn't some disaster or that something had happened to Carol. "Yeah, Dad?"

"Your friend beat me at pool."

"Oh, Jesus!"

"Watch the language, boy!"

"How'd she do that?"

"Damned if I know. I was playing good, too—I mean I wasn't easing up on her or anything just 'cause she was a female. Said her daddy taught her."

"I'll bet you were embarrassed."

Raney chuckled, which meant he was taking it better than Willie would have expected. "Let's just say it wasn't one of my shining moments."

"I wish I could've seen that."

"That's all I would've needed—my son there to witness his father's humiliation."

"You going out with her again?"

"What do you think?"

"I don't figure so."

"You figure right, Willie. When I go out with a lady, it's not to shoot pool."

"Yeah, I think Donna Lee's more your type."

"Damn right," said Raney, but for some reason he didn't sound all that convinced. Still, Willie didn't figure his father would ever want to be put in the position again of being beaten at pool by a woman.

Which was just fine with Willie, because as far as he was concerned, Carol was his.

Chapter Four

They had a stretch of Indian-summer weather about the middle of November, and then it suddenly turned cold, dropping to below freezing several nights in a row.

Willie stopped by to see Carol after football practice. He had noticed her dwindling supply of logs and figured to pick up a few extra bucks by cutting some wood for her.

As soon as he mentioned it, though, walking through her door, she nodded toward the floor, and he saw two electric heaters all plugged in and giving out more heat than the fireplace had ever managed to do.

He grinned at her. "Not one for roughing it, huh?"

"I figure living without a phone is roughing it," she told him, not even having to offer him a Coke anymore, just pointing the way to the refrigerator.

"Did you run out of logs, or do you prefer electric heat?" he asked, not wanting to give up his money-making idea so quickly.

"A fire is nice once in a while, but I'm tired of having to get up in the middle of the night to put more logs on."

He looked around the room for signs of anything new. At least once a week he noticed a few things. First the yellow stuff, then the TV, and about a week after that she had bought a cassette player. He liked her choice of music; she liked most of the same groups he liked.

He spotted the doll right away, pushed up against one of the yellow pillows on the couch. He went over and picked it up and took a good look at it. It looked just like one of the kids she was always drawing. It was a boy doll in ragged jeans and T-shirt and worn running shoes and had at least a four-inch Afro. The kid had a grin on his face and looked friendly in kind of a devious way.

"This is great," he said. "You make it?"

Carol shook her head. "They're copying them from my cards. They ought to be in the stores right after Thanksgiving."

"You make money off these?"

"Sure."

"That's neat." He put the doll back and went to get himself a Coke.

"You can have it if you want," she said.

"I'm too old for dolls."

Carol had some water on to boil, and now she was pouring it over a tea bag. He brought his Coke over to the table and sat down. When she joined him, he asked, "What are you going to do for Thanksgiving?'' He had an idea about getting her over to his house for the day.

She glanced over at her toaster oven. ''Probably go out to eat. What's a good place to get a turkey dinner?''

''I doubt any place'll be open Thanksgiving. Everyone around here eats at home, makes a big deal of it.''

''I guess I'll have a turkey TV dinner, then.''

''You can eat with us.''

''I'd just as soon eat at home, watch the game.''

''We'll be watching the game.''

''Thanks, Willie, but I'd really just as soon stay here.''

He didn't push it. He figured she didn't want to spend the day with his dad. He hadn't heard either of them mention the other since the night they'd gone to the Voyager together. He knew his father had taken a big razzing about the pool game, though. He sure wished he could've seen that.

''We're having a dance at school Saturday night after the game,'' he said.

''You going?''

''Haven't made up my mind.''

''Do you ask a date, or do you go alone, or what?''

''Mostly dates. I guess I might as well go; nothing much else to do around here on Saturday night.''

''You going to ask Linda?''

''I told you, she plays too many games. First she calls me up all the time, then she ignores me, then she tries to make me jealous.''

''Boys expect girls to play games.''

"You don't play games."

She looked surprised at that. "How do you know how I act with men?"

He shrugged. "You don't act that way with me."

"You're a friend."

He was afraid she'd say that. Not that he didn't want to be friends. "So, you mean you're like that with guys? You play games?"

"No. Not anymore. I guess I did my share of game playing in high school, though."

"So why'd you quit?" he asked, really wanting to know. He learned a lot of stuff from her when she felt like talking.

"Too much trouble; it didn't seem worth it. But one thing I did learn, though, was that the boys expected it. You just act straight with them, they don't know how to take it."

"I wouldn't mind a girl acting straight with me."

"Then act straight with them, Willie. Talk to them the way you talk to your friends."

"It wouldn't work."

"Maybe not, but why not give it a try? Isn't there any girl you'd really like to ask to the dance?"

Willie wondered what she'd say if he said he'd like to ask her. He was pretty sure that would be a mistake, though. And to be honest, if she said yes, which he knew she wouldn't, he'd feel kind of strange showing up at a school dance with a grown woman. He finally said, "I might as well ask Linda; at least I'm used to her."

"Don't any of the other girls interest you?"

He shook his head. "They're not all that different, Carol. Maybe they look a little different, but they all act the same."

"That's the thing in high school," she said. "You're supposed to act the same. If you try acting a little different, everyone thinks you're weird."

"Did they think you were weird in high school?"

She smiled. "Sometimes. When I acted like myself. I pretty much got the hang of not acting like myself after a while."

"Were you popular?"

"It's not hard to be popular, Willie. It's just a matter of blending into the crowd. You don't have to do anything to be popular; there are just a whole lot of things you can't do."

"Like what?"

She looked as if she would rather be talking about something else, and he was sorry he asked. He thought she looked a little sad for some reason, and he hoped he hadn't been the cause of it.

She said, "I guess it depends on the school. In my high school you couldn't be a tomboy and be popular."

She didn't look like his idea of a tomboy. Still and all, if she had beaten his dad at pool..."You don't look like a tomboy."

That got a smile out of her. "What does a tomboy look like?"

"I don't know—bigger, I guess."

"It's more a question of attitude than looks, Willie. If I looked the way I felt in high school, I would've been six foot tall and weighed over two hundred pounds.''

''You mean you felt like a guy?''

She considered that for a moment. ''No, not by then. When I was a little kid, I guess I did; at least I didn't feel any different than my brothers. I just meant I felt equal.''

Willie didn't feel like talking ''equality.'' They'd had that discussion before. Not that he didn't think Carol was his equal; it was just that he didn't think the girls at his school were. They all acted silly; he didn't want to feel equal to a bunch of people that went around acting silly all the time.

''I bet you were a cheerleader,'' he said to her, then was instantly sorry when he saw the look on her face. ''Guess not,'' he said, trying to make a joke of it. ''All I meant was, you're pretty enough for it.''

That didn't seem to make things any better. ''Most of the girls I know,'' he explained, ''think being a cheerleader is the greatest thing in the world.''

She seemed to relax a little so that her mouth wasn't such a straight line. ''I conformed to some extent,'' she said, ''but I drew the line at things like cheerleading.''

''I just thought—I mean, you said you were going to watch the game on Thanksgiving. I figured you must like football.''

''I like football.''

Willie figured the conversation wasn't going as well as usual and decided it might be a good idea to leave. He got up, took his empty can over to the sink, then headed for the door.

"Want to see something new I'm working on?" Carol asked him. "I wouldn't mind getting your opinion." Now she was sounding a little nervous, as if she really cared what he thought.

"Sure," he said, glad she wasn't mad at him or anything.

She went over to her drawing table and picked up a piece of drawing paper, then folded it to look like a card. She handed it to him, and he could tell she was waiting for his reaction.

It was different from her other cards, the ones with the kids. This one had an old lady sitting in a rocking chair, a hound dog at her feet and a bunch of knitting in her lap. She looked like half the old ladies in Rock Ridge, even to the apron that seemed to reside permanently around their waists. At the top of the card was printed out "Aunt Lolly says," and then under the picture it said, "If you ignore your birthdays, you won't get any older." He opened it up and read, "So ignore this card."

He felt himself smiling. It was just the kind of thing some old lady might say. "What made you do something like this?" he asked her.

"You ever read any of Mr. Rafferty's books?"

He shook his head.

"Well, I've been reading them, and they're filled with all these characters. There's one old lady, only in his book her name is Aunt Bessie, and she's always making up these words of wisdom. It just gave me the idea, that's all. I'm going to try a whole series of Aunt Lolly cards, see what my agent thinks."

"I think it's pretty funny," said Willie.

"Honest?"

She seemed to really care about getting his approval. "You want to know the truth?"

"I wouldn't ask you if I didn't."

"Well, those other cards of yours. I really like them, you know? But I doubt whether most people around here would pick out a card of a New York kid to send someone. You know what I mean? It's just that New York kids aren't familiar to us, except on TV; stuff like that. But this one. Well, I just think people around here would really like it. Everyone has some kind of Aunt Lolly in their family, you know?"

She was smiling now. "That's what I figured. Thanks. I appreciate your telling me what you think."

He was happy to see that smile. In fact, he spent most of his time with her trying to get her to smile. He hoped she wasn't thinking about cheerleaders anymore.

SHE WAS STARTING to get stir-crazy again.

For a while the TV had helped, but Carol had never been a big TV watcher, and after the novelty wore off, she couldn't stand ninety percent of what she watched.

She bought the cassette player and a bunch of cassettes, but just sitting around and listening to music didn't interest her. She liked to hear music when she was working, but it didn't entertain her all by itself.

She was still doing a lot of reading, and she found that what she enjoyed reading the most was Mr. Rafferty's books. They were filled with continuing characters, and she surmised that they were based on real people from Rock Ridge. She hadn't got the idea for

the card series right away. It was only after she found
herself sketching some of his characters that the idea
came to her. She wasn't at all sure the idea would appeal to her agent, who was a pretty sophisticated New
Yorker, but she thought it was worth a try. She was
getting to a point with her street kids where it was hard
coming up with new ideas. She needed a change.

This renewed her interest in her work, and for a
while she didn't find a need for any other form of en-
tertainment, but after Willie left that day, she started
to think about going to the Voyager again.

She had liked Donna Lee and had appreciated her
offer of saving a seat for her. The trouble was, Donna
Lee wouldn't be the only one at the bar. Raney was
sure to be there, too, and she wasn't sure she wanted
to run into him again. She hadn't been unaware of
how he had felt losing at pool to her. Her brothers had
never minded, but then they always took some of the
credit for giving her pointers when she was learning.
Other guys didn't like it, though, as she had found out
in school on the couple of occasions she had shot pool
with the boys.

School. Willie had got her thinking about high
school, a period of her life she wasn't in the least nos-
talgic about. She had been popular, as she told him.
It was just that being popular meant being unhappy.
It meant dressing in a way she didn't want to dress,
acting totally different from what was natural for her
and always being afraid to really loosen up in case her
real self came out. Most of the time she succeeded.
Sometimes, though, she got tired of playing the end-
less games and just said or did what came naturally,

which made her come out looking as if she had some kind of split personality.

She guessed she did have a split personality in those days. There was the way she had been before her father left and then the way she became after that.

In retrospect, she could understand a lot now that she hadn't understood at the time. At the time, at age twelve, all she could understand was that her dad had left her. And her dad comprised almost all of her world.

She had been his favorite. Oh, he loved his three older sons, too, but he had been absolutely crazy about Carol. He had managed to treat her like a fourth son and also make her feel special. Now, thinking back on it, maybe it had been because she hadn't been her mother's favorite; if her mother had had her way, she would've managed to make Carol feel inadequate.

Even as a child she had sensed her mother was jealous of the attention her father gave her. Her mother had resorted to acting cute, talking baby talk to him, even though Carol had never done either. She preferred her sons, who learned early that flirting with her got the best results. They all called her their "girl," which Carol's mother adored. But then she was a girl who never really did grow up. For all Carol knew, she still hadn't.

Carol understood other things now, though. She understood that her mother was a product of her own parents, who had spoiled her and kept her like a child. She understood that her mother's parents had never approved of her father and hadn't wanted their only daughter to marry a high-school football coach who would never be able to support her the way they had supported her. She understood that they did everything in their power to undermine the marriage. And finally they succeeded.

All Carol understood at age twelve was that her father took a job coaching college football and moved to California without them.

Carol, who had been something of a street kid herself, used to her neighborhood in Chicago, able to defend herself in fights with the boys, having grown up with her father taking her to the Cubs games in the summer and the Bears games during the football season, thinking of home as a small, noisy apartment, was in for a second shock. Her mother, four children in tow, promptly moved back into her parents' house in Evanston.

It was a big house on the lake, but it was never a home. Her brothers adjusted quickly. The two older ones got cars of their own, and all three of them took to boating on the lake. Their grandfather even interested them in golf, which Carol was convinced was a sissy game. At least that's what her father always called it. In vain, she waited to hear from her father, determined to run away and join him. But a letter never came.

It was bad enough having her father leave. It was bad enough having a mother who was suddenly dating and seldom around. What was the very worst was that her grandmother took over the mothering, which meant trying to reshape Carol into her mother's mold, into being what her grandmother termed a "lady." She resisted the attempts all through junior high, sneaking out of the house to play football, ditching ballet classes, keeping her jeans and sneakers at a friend's house to change into, learning to lie and mostly get away with it.

By high school her strong-willed grandmother wore her down; that and the fact that the boys no longer regarded her as one of them and started treating her different. That's when the real Carol went underground and a more socially acceptable Carol came to the fore—a Carol who was popular, who learned how to flirt with boys, to gossip with girls, to curl her hair and apply makeup and to shop for the right clothes.

She would never know whether she might have found herself in college and become her own person again. Instead, and incurring the wrath of her grandparents until the day they died, she went off on her own to New York and worked in an office during the day while taking art courses at night. And she had never been sorry once.

She kept in contact with Mark, the brother closest in age to her. Through him she learned of her father's remarriage and of his new family. She learned of her mother's two subsequent marriages and divorces and of her brother's marriages and children. She was the odd one, the only woman in the family with a career. Just once she wrote to her father. He sent her a Christmas card that year with a picture of his new wife and two daughters on it and on the back a note saying how pleased he was to hear from her.

By that time she knew that her father hadn't deserted them. Her brother had told her that her mother had refused to go along with him when he got a better job on the Coast. He also told her that her father had written to her but that her grandparents thought the letters would be too upsetting to her and they had destroyed them. Still, despite the explanations, she felt deserted. If her father had loved her as much as he always had seemed to love her, she didn't see how he could've just left that way. She would never understand it.

She learned to be a loner, to depend only on herself. And it worked. Not only worked, but she was convinced it was the only way to live. She didn't need a shrink to tell her she was living defensively, that if she didn't love someone, then she couldn't be left and thus hurt. She realized that about herself; in fact, she planned it that way.

She didn't dislike men. She had grown up with boys, had always felt the most comfortable with boys. It was just that she liked them up to a point. And that point was when they started making moves on her.

She had hated the New York men she had met. They hadn't even seemed like men to her. They were all into health clubs and designer clothes and styled hair and spent as much time thinking and talking about those things as the women did. They were into playing games with women, too. They were just like high-school boys who had taken it a step further.

And, of course, she compared each one to what she remembered of her father, and they came out lacking.

She often wondered how Willie felt about his mother deserting him. She kept hoping he would bring up the subject so that they could compare notes, but he never did. Maybe one of these days she would tell him about her father and see if he responded.

She was crazy about Willie, but occasioanlly she felt like adult companionship. Just someone to talk to. She decided she would go to the Voyager that night. If Raney was there, that was his problem, not hers. She would just have a couple of beers with Donna Lee, a little conversation, then head on home.

No reason to get a reputation as a recluse.

RANEY, who had about given up on Donna Lee and was planning on stopping at the Voyager just long enough to get a buzz on and then head over to Maybelle's house, did a double take when he saw Carol seated at the bar with Donna Lee, the two of them laughing and talking like old friends.

He was starting to head for the other side of the bar when Donna Lee spotted him and waved him over. He reversed his course and decided that if she even mentioned the word "pool," he was going to head right out of the bar.

"Raney, honey," said Donna Lee, "you-all are coming over for Thanksgiving, aren't you?"

"Wouldn't miss it," he said.

Then Raney heard her add, "Carol just promised to come over," and he wished he had bitten his tongue. Oh, well, the house would be filled with Donna Lee's brothers and sisters and their families, and at least Willie would be pleased to see his friend there.

"I don't want to crowd you," Carol was saying.

But Donna Lee just laughed and said, "One more person? Tell her what a raft of people there's going to be, Raney."

"Donna Lee's a great cook," he told her. "You, wouldn't want to miss it."

Donna Lee turned to Raney. "She was afraid she'd miss the game. I told her I couldn't even remember a Thanksgiving without a football game on the TV, although I wouldn't mind."

"You like football?" he asked Carol, wondering why he was surprised. Anyone who played pool that well probably knew her football, too.

She didn't say anything, just nodded. He knew she had been talking a streak when he walked in, and Willie swore she did a lot of talking. Maybe it was just he who shut her up.

As usual, Donna Lee was looking sharp, this time in a pink wool pantsuit with black trim, and as usual, Carol was dressed a little strange. The jeans were okay. The running shoes were okay, he supposed. On top, though, she was wearing some kind of flannel blazer in large black-and-white checks that went clear to her knees and had enormous shoulder pads, and under that was a T-shirt with Save the Whales printed on it. He wondered if everyone in New York dressed as she did.

"I was thinking, Raney," Donna Lee was saying to him, "maybe we ought to introduce Carol to Delbert."

Carol gave her a questioning look, and Donna Lee said, "Delbert McClure; he teaches art over at the high school."

"And is as queer as a—" began Raney before he was punched in the arm by Donna Lee.

"He's no such thing, Raney Catlin, and you got no call saying that. He was seeing Betty Sue Ostrey a while back, and from what I hear he was man enough for her."

"It doesn't matter; I'm really not interested," said Carol, and both of them looked at her.

"You two'd have a lot in common, honey," said Donna Lee.

"Far as I know, Delbert don't shoot pool," said Raney, inadvertently bringing up the one subject he had hoped to avoid.

He got a smile out of Carol.

"I tell you what," said Donna Lee. "I'll invite him over Thanksgiving, and you can make up your mind then."

"Please," said Carol, keeping her voice low, "you don't have to introduce me to men. I'm really not interested, honest."

"You keep saying that, but it isn't normal. Is it, Raney?"

It didn't sound normal to Raney, but whether Carol met men or didn't meet men didn't really interest him much. He could see Donna Lee's mind going a mile a minute, though, and decided to do Carol a favor and change the subject. "Hear about the strike down at the plant?" he asked Donna Lee.

She nodded. "Doesn't affect you, though, does it?"

Raney shook his head. "No, the drivers are a different union."

Donna Lee turned to Carol. "You ever seen any of the furniture Raney's made?"

Carol shook her head.

"He's got a real talent for it. Furniture plant closed down, though; now Raney's driving a truck for the carpet place. About the only industry left around here."

"I don't mind it. I like to move around," said Raney.

"Remind me to show you on Thanksgiving," said Donna Lee. "He built us a breakfront that's a work of art. A real work of art."

"I'd like to see it," said Carol, and Raney knew she was just being polite.

"You ought to have him show you his house," said Donna Lee. "He built most of the furniture himself."

Carol didn't say she'd like to see that, and Raney found himself grinning. He could read them both like a book. Now Donna Lee had switched from promoting Delbert to promoting him, and Carol was no doubt wishing she had stayed at home. He almost felt sorry enough for her to offer to shoot her a game of pool. Hell, he ought to, anyway. Best thing to shut the guys up. He bet they all figured he'd never get near a pool table with her again.

"Want to shoot a game?" he heard himself asking, not really expecting her to say yes.

But he was not really surprised when she slid off the stool and said, "Why not?"

"I'm sorry about that," she said to him on the way to the back room. "Donna Lee seems to think I need a man."

"What do you think?"

She grinned up at him. "I think I'm doing just fine without one."

That was okay for her, but he wasn't doing so fine without a woman. He thought about Maybelle and decided to make it a fast game.

They were only a couple of minutes into the game and it was about even when Marcie put her head through the door and said the cops were on the phone and wanted to talk to him.

"What've you done now, Raney?" one of the guys yelled out, but Carol didn't say anything; she didn't even look at him.

"Be right back," he said to her, knowing there was nothing the cops would want him for but having a pretty good idea that Willie and his friends had been caught with a can of beer in a truck or some such thing.

Just what he needed. He'd skin the kid if he prevented him from getting over to see Maybelle.

It was Billy Grogan down at the jail. "Got your boy down here, Raney," he was told.

"What's the charge, Billy?"

"Caught a few of them climbing the old water tower."

Raney almost laughed out loud. "You mean the same one we used to climb, Billy?"

There was a pause; then Billy said, "It's trespassing, Raney. Plus it's dangerous. Thing's about to fall down."

Raney thought of Maybelle. "Let him spend the night cooling off in jail, why don't you?"

"You don't want the kid to get a record, Raney. We just wanted to throw a scare in them. The kid driving had a couple of beers. We're just asking the parents to come down and pick them up, that's all."

Damn kid was going to mess up his evening any way he looked at it.

Back in the pool room he told Carol he had to go down to the jail and pick up Willie. He saw the concern on her face and said, "No big deal. They didn't arrest him or nothing."

"You seem upset," she said, which was perhaps the first personal thing she had ever said to him.

"For messing up my evening, that's all. I had a date in a little while; probably miss it now."

"I'll pick him up for you if you want."

He stood there considering her offer, almost going for it. But no, Willie was his responsibility, not hers. "Appreciate it, but I better go myself. Kid needs to be taught a lesson."

She sounded a little hesitant when she asked, "Can I go along?"

He figured why not; the evening was shot, anyway. "Yeah, come on along. Give you a chance to see our local jail," he said with a grin.

He waited while she got her jacket off the bar stool and said something to Donna Lee; then she followed him out to his truck. "Want to take my car?" she asked him.

"No need."

"I just thought there'd be more room."

He paused. "Yeah, okay. Maybe you could drop me off back here and drive Willie on home."

She nodded and unlocked the door of the passenger seat for him. He got inside and immediately smelled the new leather. Nice car, good-looking interior. He couldn't remember the last time he'd driven in anything but a pickup truck.

It made him nervous driving with a woman, but she drove okay, one arm out the window, even though it was chilly out, the other hand resting lightly on the steering wheel. She seemed so concentrated on her driving that he was surprised when she said, "What'd he do?"

"Climbed a water tower."

She looked over at him, her smile kind of half in place. "That's all?"

"Well, you know—not much crime in a small place like this, so they hassle the kids."

"I climbed a few water towers when I was a kid."

"Yeah, so did I."

"I used to like the feeling of being up high like that."

He remembered. Just kidding around, he said, "Want to find us a water tower and climb it?"

She looked over at him, then did a double take. "You think I wouldn't?"

He chuckled. "I reckon you would. You ever been arrested?"

She was nodding. "A couple of times. When I was a kid."

"What'd you do?"

"Once for breaking a window of a school; we were playing baseball. The other time we snuck in Soldier's Field and got caught by the watchman."

"Soldier's Field?"

"In Chicago. Where the Bears play."

"Regular juvenile delinquent."

"What about you?"

"I got in my share of trouble. Best time was when we stole some of the local moonshiner's product. He couldn't rightly call the cops on us, of course, but when his sons caught us, they scared hell out of us."

He leaned forward now and directed her to where the jail was, then opened the door of the car as soon as she parked at the curb. "I'll just be a minute," he told her.

Billy Grogan, about fifty pounds heavier than he had been in high school and all of it in the stomach, was grinning when Raney walked in. "Sorry to drag you away from your pool game," he told Raney.

Raney figured from the big grin that Billy knew just who he had been playing with and how she had beat him the first time. "You dragged me away from more than that, Billy; supposed to see Maybelle later on."

"I figure you'll still make that, Raney."

Raney figured so, too. To tell the truth, he was getting out of the mood, but then you didn't necessarily need to be in the mood for Maybelle. Maybelle had ways of getting you in the mood.

Willie, looking half scared and half defiant, was led out by one of Billy's deputies, and Raney made sure the kid heard the big sigh and noted the put-upon look Raney was giving him. There were proper times for parents to act like martyrs, and this was one of them.

"All we did, Dad—" Willie started to explain when they got outside.

But Raney shut him up with "I don't want to hear no excuses, boy," and then he was watching the way Willie's face lit up when he saw Carol waiting for them in her car.

SHE COULD REMEMBER the time when her father had to come down to the juvenile detention center and picked her up when she and her friends had been caught sneaking into Soldier's Field. They hadn't been caught instantly; they'd been able to get in a little football practice before the watchman with the shotgun had showed up. It had been exciting—worth it— being able to play where the pros played.

Her dad hadn't said anything to her while they were still inside getting her signed out; he had just cocked an eyebrow in her direction and then rolled his eyes. Anyway, she wasn't scared—not of the police and not of her father. She didn't figure what she did was all that bad.

He took her outside to the old Pontiac he had driven for as long as she could remember, and once inside the car, his first words were "How did it feel?"

"Great. Like Joe Namath."

She figured that would get a rise out of him, but he just chuckled. She knew he thought she was a traitor for deserting the Bears in favor of the Jets, but the Bears never won, and she was tired of losing teams.

"You don't want to get yourself a police record, honey."

"I wouldn't mind," she said, acting tough. She thought it would be cool to have a police record. Some of the older boys in the neighborhood—ones in high school—had them and the rest of the kids really respected them.

"You'd mind. Your mother would have you sent off to a private girls' school so fast you wouldn't know what hit you."

The old threat but an effective one. Carol couldn't think of a worse punishment than having to go to a girls' school. "Were you ever arrested when you were a kid?" she asked her dad.

"When I was your age, I was working to help support the family," he said.

She had heard it about a million times and it still didn't answer her question. "But didn't you ever have any adventures?"

But if he had, he didn't admit to any. Any more than she figured Raney was going to admit to Willie that he had ever climbed water towers. If she had kids, she'd be different. She'd tell them the truth when they asked her, not try to come across as some wise adult who never did anything wrong.

Willie was grinning when he saw her, and she grinned back. "Broke up our pool game, kid," she said to him, noticing the look she got from Raney when she said it.

"Yeah? Who was winning?"

She caught another look from Raney, but she just said, "No one was winning; we had just got started."

She headed back for the bar, and there was silence in the car, and then Willie said, "Heard you're pretty good at pool."

"Where I grew up, you had to be."

"Girls?" He sounded disbelieving.

"Well, maybe not girls, but I hung around with boys."

"Carol was a tomboy, Dad," said Willie.

Randy said, "I could've figured that out for myself."

Carol figured that if she didn't bring up the matter of the water tower, Raney would leave it until later and really give Willy hell, so she decided she would bring it out in the open and dissipate some of the tension she felt between them. "Which water tower were you climbing?" she asked him. She had noticed three in the area.

"That old one near the high school. It's not used anymore."

She was nodding, remembering. That was one she wouldn't care to climb herself. It looked as if just a soft breeze would crumble it.

"Damn fool thing to do," said Raney, looking back over the seat at his son.

"We didn't see any cops around."

"I don't mean getting caught," said Raney. "I meant climbing it in the first place. Thing's falling apart."

"It held six of us," said Willie, really asking for it, thought Carol.

"You being a wise mouth, boy?"

"No, sir."

"How do you think I would've felt being called out of the bar to be told you was dead?"

Willie was silent.

Raney turned around in the seat and stared straight ahead. Carol glanced over in time to see him light a cigarette, his hands shaking.

"You ever climb a water tower, Dad?"

Carol was expecting an immediate no. Instead, Raney said, "Not a broken-down one like that. I had some brains, boy."

Carol looked over at Raney and caught his eye. She couldn't help it; she tried not to, but she started to laugh, anyway. Then Raney started to laugh. Willie, who probably couldn't figure out what they were laughing about, finally joined them, and they were still laughing when Carol turned into the parking lot of the Voyager.

"Call you at midnight, Willie," Raney told him as he opened the car door.

"You staying out all night, Dad?"

Raney looked at Carol. "Maybe I ought to take him on home myself. You might want to stay at the Voyager a little longer."

"That's okay; I'm ready to go home," said Carol.

Raney gave a nod. "See you later, then."

Carol drove off before he could change his mind.

Chapter Five

Carol's earliest memories of Thanksgiving were of having to get dressed up in a fancy dress and fancy shoes and then being crowded into the car for the long drive up to Wilmette to her cousins' house. These were the rich cousins, her mother's side of the family.

When she was little, a fuss was always made over her because she was the only girl in the family. She was expected to be cute and sweet and, above all, clean, which prevented her from joining in, in the games her brothers and her cousins played in the backyard and relegated her to the house with the grown-ups.

When she hit about the age of eight, she rebelled. She would go out in the yard and join the boys even if it meant getting her dress torn or her shoes dirty, and when her mother or her grandmother would make a fuss and insist she behave like a girl, her daddy would stand up for her and tell them to leave her be. Along about then she stopped being their "darling little girl" and started to become either a "problem child" or the "black sheep of the family," depending on who was talking about her. She didn't care. She had never wanted to be anyone's darling little girl.

In high school she went back to conforming. By that time two of her brothers and all of her cousins were in college. They would show up for holiday dinners just long enough to eat, then cut out to see their friends. There were no longer games in the backyard. Carol would sit around, trying to keep her mouth shut and not get into any trouble, the only highlight of the day being the football game, which she would watch in the den with her uncle.

Thanksgivings in New York had been a joy. She could go to the movies, she could go out for pizza, she could just stay home and eat peanut butter sandwiches, and there was no one to tell her that wasn't the way to behave. Mostly, though, holidays didn't mean very much to her anymore, since she worked at home and one day was pretty much like any other.

If she had known a polite way to do it, she would have got out of going to Donna Lee's for Thanksgiving. But she liked the woman and would not have wanted to hurt her feelings. Anyway, Donna Lee seemed to accept her the way she was.

She had turned down Raney's offer, relayed through Willie, to drive over with them. She preferred having her own transportation in case she wanted to leave early. Willie had given her directions to Donna Lee's house, and Carol, not knowing what was expected of guests in Rock Ridge, had bought a pound of chocolates and gathered up a bunch of pussy willows to take over to Donna Lee.

She wore camel wool pants and a brown cashmere sweater and a heavy tweed blazer with a little tweed cap on her head, which was about as dressed up as her clothes got, and decided she looked a combination of English and preppy, which ought to do for the occasion. What she didn't look was "pretty," which is how her mother and grandmother always wanted her to look and the way most of the women in Rock Ridge tried to look. She still had a thing against conforming.

Donna Lee had told her to come any time in the afternoon, and Carol had planned on arriving just in time for the football game, but she was ready early and got tired of walking around the small confines of the cabin with nothing to do until she went, so finally she just got into her car and headed over to Donna Lee's house.

When she got there, she found cars parked all over Donna Lee's front lawn, or what would have been a front lawn if so many cars hadn't worn it away to just dirt. She pulled hers up into an available space and got out, avoiding the muddy patches as best she could.

The front door was ajar, and when no one heard her knock, she pushed it open and went inside. The house looked fairly large from the outside; inside it seemed filled with people. Kids of all ages and assorted adults were everywhere, but thankfully Donna Lee spotted her and came right over. When Donna Lee reached out to kiss her cheek, Carol caught herself from flinching just in time and instead accepted the kiss. She had become proficient as a child at avoiding the kisses of relatives, but Donna Lee was just being friendly, and Carol didn't want to insult her. Donna Lee took the candy and pussy willows and made a big fuss over them, then led Carol into what she termed the parlor and started introducing her around.

The women were all more dressed up than Carol, but the men were less, and the kids wore a motley assortment of clothes. She shook a lot of hands and tried to remember names, but for some reason all the people looked so much alike she had trouble differentiating them. She looked around for Willie for someone to talk to but didn't see either him or Raney.

"Can I help you with anything?" she asked Donna Lee, thinking that hiding out in the kitchen would be preferable to trying to fit into a family gathering.

But Donna Lee didn't come through. She just said, "Not a thing. You just set yourself down and enjoy yourself, honey."

Carol was asked the same two questions by a lot people. The first one was "Hear you're from New York, that right?" and she would say, "Yes," and that would be the end of that. The second one was "You're the lady does those cards, right?" and she would nod her head, and then he or she would say, "Fancy that," or words to that effect, and then turn to someone else.

The women were perpetually up and down chasing kids, and when they were down, they were talking about kids. The men were drinking beer and talking about work. Except for the initial two questions, meant, she supposed, to place her, Carol was smiled at occasionally by the women and ignored by the men, and when she saw a boy of about twelve head for the back door with a football under his arm, she got up and looked out a back window to see what was happening outside.

She felt like a little kid again when she saw the boys getting up a game of football in the back while she was stuck in the house with the adults. She figured she wouldn't be breaking any rules by going outside and watching them, so she went out the back door and closed it softly behind her.

She was standing there watching the kids twenty minutes later when Willie came out of the house and stopped when he saw her. "What're you doing out here?" he wanted to know.

"Just getting some air."

"Talk to you later," he said, running to get into the game.

She thought about going inside and being sociable, then decided to give it another few minutes. She doubted she would be missed.

When Raney came out, he looked from her to the game. She expected him to make some wise remark, but instead he smiled a slow smile and said, "Wishing you were a kid again and could join in?"

"No," she said, too quickly and too adamantly, judging by the expression on his face.

"Delbert's arrived. Donna Lee sent me to find you."

"Delbert?"

The smile turned to a grin. "The art teacher; the one Donna Lee's fixing to set you up with."

"I thought she was kidding about that."

"Donna Lee doesn't kid when it comes to men."

Carol saw that he was as amused by it as she was, but she had been outside long enough, anyway. Any longer and it would be bordering on rude. "Might as well get it over with," she said, taking one last look at the game before following him inside. At least Delbert would be another outsider, maybe someone to talk to.

Actually, Delbert wasn't that bad. About her own age, rather nice-looking and sounding more educated than the rest. Or maybe it was just that he didn't have as strong an accent so she didn't have to listen so closely to his words. He was even dressed rather like her in the same kind of tweed jacket.

He asked her about her work, and she asked him about his teaching, and at one point he asked if she would come to the school one day and explain to his art classes what she was doing.

"I'd be glad to," she told him, thinking it might be fun.

"I'll set up a day, then, and let you know. Got a phone number?"

"I don't have a phone. You know Willie Catlin?"

"Sure, I know all the kids."

"Well, you can send a message through him. He's my nearest neighbor."

She found she was enjoying talking to him and hardly noticed when all the men got up and began filing out of the room until Raney stopped by her chair.

"Is it time for dinner?" she asked him.

"The game's coming on," he said. "Thought you'd want to know."

"You going to watch the game?" she asked Delbert.

He shrugged indifferently. "Makes no difference."

"I'd like to see it," she told him, getting up. He got up, too, and they followed Raney down some stairs into a basement where a TV set and some outdoor furniture were set up.

The men had already taken all the chairs, and Carol sat down cross-legged on a braided rug on the floor. Right away one of the men got up and offered her a chair, but she said, "No, thanks," and stayed where she was. As the only woman there, she wasn't about to demand privileges.

Raney was tuning in the TV set, and one of the men said, "Hey, Raney, she'd make someone a good wife. Doesn't even mind watching a football game on Thanksgiving."

"Yeah, but who'd be in the kitchen fixing dinner?" said Raney, getting a big laugh from the men.

She saw Delbert leaning against the wall and assumed he didn't want to get his trousers dirty. The rug was pretty dirty, full of cat hair or dog hair, although she hadn't noticed any pets around, but she didn't feel like standing for three hours, and clothes could be cleaned.

They turned out to be a vociferous bunch of men. They discussed every play, argued every penalty called and were constantly apologizing to her for their language after the fact. She just kept quiet and concentrated on the game and tried to be as unobtrusive as possible, but she had a feeling she was cramping their style just by being there.

During halftime, Raney went upstairs and came back down carrying two folding chairs that he sat up for her and Delbert, and she got up off the floor gratefully, her rear end practically numb at that point.

Carol noticed that Delbert was in the best shape of any of the men there and attributed it to his not having a wife to feed him. The other men wore their pants low, their bellies hanging out over the waistband, not even attempting to suck in their guts. To be fair, Raney was in pretty good shape. Better than the other men, and if Delbert looked in better shape, it was probably because he was slim to begin with.

Mostly the talk revolved around football during halftime, but at one point one of the men said to Delbert, "Haven't seen you in a coon's age, Del."

Delbert said, "Keeping busy, R.T. Felt lucky to get an invite over here, get a home-cooked meal."

Raney, with an evil glint in his eyes, said, "That wasn't an invite; that was a setup." And when Delbert looked puzzled, Raney said, "Donna Lee's fixin' to set up you and Carol here."

"Oh, I don't think so," said Delbert, suddenly looking very uncomfortable.

"I'm afraid he's right, Delbert," Carol said. "At the time I thought she was just kidding, but..." She shrugged and gave him a smile.

"Not that I mind," said Delbert, getting a laugh from the men and leaving Carol feeling suddenly uncomfortable. Not that she was worried about Delbert. She knew his type, and she'd scare the hell out of him if he got to know her.

Then, as though Carol were now placed in the proper context and the men understood why she was there, they loosened up a little and started talking to her. One of them asked her if she was the pool hustler he'd heard about, and Carol said, "I don't recall hustling," and then another one asked if she really liked football, or was she just hiding out from the women.

"I really like it," Carol assured him, and when he still looked doubtful, she said, "My dad coached high-school football when I was a kid. I grew up with it."

"You really shoot pool?" Delbert asked her, sounding as though he was sure it was all a joke.

"Sure, don't you?" she countered.

"Yes," he said, making it sound like "Of course." "I just don't know any women who do."

"Gotta watch out for those northern women," said one of the men, getting a few laughs.

"I'd be glad to shoot pool with you sometime," Delbert offered.

But before Carol could say anything, one of the men said, "I hear Raney's got a monopoly on that."

"The hell he does," Carol said, getting a laugh herself.

After that she was practically one of the boys, and they even included her in their football talk. All except Delbert, who wasn't participating in the football talk, and Raney, who seemed to be put out for some reason by what she had said.

RANEY LIKED the way she handled herself. Any other woman he knew would've acted coy when he made that remark to Delbert about it being a setup. Of course, any other woman he knew wouldn't have been down in the basement with the men to begin with. Her father being a football coach accounted for that, though; talking football was probably second nature to her.

He'd got a little annoyed when the talk had turned to pool and old Delbert had offered to play her. Hell, he didn't think Delbert had been near a pool table in a good ten years. And when he had been near one, he had hardly known which end of the stick to use. He'd get a real surprise if he thought Carol was going to be his kind of competition. And she sure as hell wasn't the kind of woman who was going to let a man win just to bolster his ego.

If she wanted to shoot pool, he'd shoot with her. Why not? She was better competition than what he usually got, and he didn't have one of those ego problems.

And speaking of problems, he noticed she had no problem talking to Delbert. Didn't even have a problem joining in the football talk once she was made to feel welcome. He still had a problem talking to her, though, so it must be him. He just couldn't remember ever having a problem talking to anyone before.

Course they had nothing in common to talk about except Willie. Maybe if he had some problem with Willie, he could stop by her place and discuss it with her.

Except—wait a minute here—who said he even wanted to talk to her? He wasn't that hard up for a woman that he had to go after someone totally not his type at all. Well, to be honest, he was pretty hard up. But she didn't seem like the kind of woman you used. She didn't even seem like the kind of woman who'd be remotely interested.

She seemed sexless; that was the thing. Kind of neuter. She just didn't have any womanly traits about her. Delbert didn't appear to agree with him, and Willie sure as hell liked her, but what did either of them really know about women when it came right down to it?

He kept his eye on her during the second half of the game. She joined in the conversation now and then, twice calling a penalty before any of the men got it. So she knew football. So what? All his buddies knew football. And it wasn't a buddy he was looking for.

She did have a cute little face, particularly beneath the cap she was wearing. Those big dark eyes, that determined mouth—it was a tomboyish face, appealing. The thing was, it wasn't the kind of face that made him want to kiss it; it was more the kind of face where he felt like taking off her cap and tousling her hair. *Forget it, Raney,* he told himself, *she isn't for you; the appeal just isn't there.*

And then he saw her turn and her face light up in one of those smiles of hers, and he saw it was Willie who was making her smile. He watched as his son sat down at her feet and the way the two of them were all of a sudden talking as if they'd known each other all their lives. And for no reason at all he wished he could get her to talk to him that way. Just once, anyway; just once, to see what it felt like.

Oh, hell—What was he thinking? Women weren't for talking to, except maybe a little sweet talk in the beginning. Women were for loving and taking care of and maybe just looking at when you wanted to look at something good. That was probably what she needed, anyway—a little loving, a little taking care of, something to turn her into a real woman.

She was still a kid; that was her problem. Watching her talk to Willie, he could see they were two of a kind, both kids. That's why Willie was so big on her; they were just alike in that respect. She might have lived thirty years, according to Willie, but he would bet that tomboy was still residing inside her just dying to get out.

Some shouting brought him out of his reverie, and he noted, to his chagrin, that all that deep thinking had caused him to miss a touchdown. Hell, no woman was worth that.

WILLIE WOULD HAVE LIKED to sit next to Carol at dinner, for he sensed she was feeling ill at ease in the gathering, but as usual, the kids were relegated to the picnic table in the kitchen, while the adults filled the large table in the dining room.

His father had taken over the duties of the man of the house and carved the turkey, and Willie had noticed that he hadn't made a big deal of it as he sometimes did. Sometimes his dad really liked being center stage, and that embarrassed Willie. He remembered it embarrassing his mother, too, and then he remembered he didn't want to think about his mother, so he stopped.

The best part about the kids all eating together was that no one was there to say, "Eat all your stringbeans," or, "Use your fork, not your fingers," and when Matty, who was fourteen, tried something like that on her little brother, all the rest of the kids threw mashed potatoes at her. He had to give Matty credit, though. She didn't run to Donna Lee and complain; she just wiped the potatoes off her face and stopped trying to come on like a mother.

As usual, all the adults stuffed themselves so much they decided to prolong dessert for an hour, which didn't set well with the kids, but they weren't given any choice.

Willie wandered into the parlor to see what was happening, and he could tell just by the expression on her face that Carol was trying to think of a way to get out of there without even waiting for dessert.

"Hey, Carol," he said to her, "why don't you show the kids how you can draw?"

"I don't think they'd be interested, Willie," she said, but at least it wasn't an outright no.

"Sure they would. You could sketch them, like you've sketched me. They'd love it."

"If you want," she said, and he went off and borrowed some paper and a felt-tip pen from Matty, then told all the kids what was happening.

The women had cleared off the picnic table by then, and Willie got all the kids back, except a couple who were watching TV in the basement, and Carol sat down and started doing quick sketches of them one by one. Only they weren't exact sketches like the ones she'd done of him. Instead, she'd exaggerate some part of them. Like Donny, who always had this big smile on his face; she made his smile so wide it almost reached to his ears. The kids thought the exaggerations were real funny.

Then a couple of the ladies saw what was happening and wanted their pictures drawn, so as soon as she had done all the kids, Carol started in on them. He noticed with them, though, that she didn't do any exaggeration, which was just as well, or she probably would have made them all real fat.

Then the men noticed what was going on in the kitchen, probably because someone hadn't brought them a beer, but none of them asked to be drawn until Mr. McClure showed up. Willie didn't especially like one of the teachers seeing him in real life. In fact, he couldn't figure out why Mr. McClure was even there. He hadn't known he was any particular friend of Donna Lee's.

"How about one of me?" Mr. McClure asked Carol, and she took a clean sheet of paper and told him to stand still.

The head looked like Mr. McClure, all right, but then she drew in one of those berets on his head like Frenchmen wore and hung a big, floppy bow around his neck.

"The artist as teacher. Is that how you see me?" said Mr. McClure, and when she nodded, he smiled and said it was very good, then carefully rolled it up to keep.

And then his dad, whom he hadn't even seen come into the room, said, "How do you see me?"

Carol looked up at him. "You sure you want to know?"

Raney saw that stopped his dad for a second, but then he said, "Why not?"

Carol got another piece of paper, and without even telling him to stand still or even looking at him, she quickly sketched his dad leaning over a pool table, cue stick in hand and a determined look on his face.

"I guess I asked for that," said his dad, kind of smiling, but Willie noticed he left the picture where it was on the table. Later, though, Willie took it and folded it up to keep.

CAROL FOUND that she had truly enjoyed most of the day. She had expected it to be an ordeal, but it hadn't been at all. What had really surprised her was how well everyone got along. There were grandparents and parents and children and aunts and uncles and in-laws, and except for a little good-natured bickering, mostly among the children, everyone was pleasant to everyone else. In contrast, her family had always been outwardly polite, but there was always a definite subtext to everything said.

When she saw mothers start to gather up their children to leave, Carol went to Donna Lee and told her what a lovely time she had had and thanked her for inviting her.

"Oh, honey, I was glad you came. Wasn't as bad as you thought it would be, was it?"

Carol couldn't help smiling. "I was afraid, not knowing anyone..."

"It's nice to have new faces around. Tell me, how'd you hit it off with Delbert?"

"He's very nice."

Donna Lee grinned. "That he is, but not too exciting, right?"

"I doubt he found me exciting, either, Donna Lee."

"Raney's a good man, you know."

Carol was startled at the change of subject. "Raney?"

"Yes, Raney. Oh, I know he comes on a little strong, but the man has a good heart."

"Raney's not interested in me."

"Well, Raney's looking for a woman, and he could sure do a lot worse."

"I've told you, Donna Lee, I'm not looking for a man."

"So you keep telling me, sweetie, but to me those words are like a foreign language."

Carol, knowing she'd never convince her, didn't pursue it. But on the way home she thought about the couples there and about her father and his new family and her mother and her marriages and her brothers' families and wondered why she was different. She had to wonder why she didn't miss that kind of closeness, but she really didn't think she did.

She had kept the men in her life pretty compartmentalized. There had been some, particularly in her art-school days, who had been friends of hers. They had gone to museums together and galleries and often to movies, but the friendships had never developed romantically. Then there had been a few men over the years she had been interested in romantically, but she had never felt they were friends and had prevented any real closeness from developing.

Never once in her life had she allowed a man to spend an entire night with her, and more than once this had precipitated the eventual breakup. She felt that having sex with a man was one thing; waking up with him in the morning was quite a another. She was sure that after spending an entire night, moving in with her would come next, and after that, worse. Worse being either marriage or leaving her; she wasn't sure which.

After just meeting him once, she knew that Delbert was the kind of man she could be friends with. She would enjoy talking art with him, going to movies together, just hanging out once in a while. Physcially, he didn't appeal to her at all. But then the kind of men who should appeal to her physically never did.

She couldn't even understand why Donna Lee had brought up Raney, except maybe she was trying to get him off her own back. It wasn't that he didn't appeal to her physically; he would probably appeal to most women physically. His attitude toward women, though, more than offset any physical appeal he might have. She didn't blame him for his attitude. All the men she had met in Rock Ridge seemed to have exactly the same attitude toward women. She, however, wasn't a southern woman. She didn't want to be treated like a child, to be taken care of. She wanted to be treated as an equal, and that appeared to be poison to a southern man.

It wasn't a problem, anyway. Even if she spent the full year in Rock Ridge, she had gone longer than that without a man, and it had never bothered her. She was working well, enjoying the quiet for the most part and experiencing a totally new way of life, which was always good for her creativity.

Men didn't even have to enter into the picture.

Chapter Six

Willie had been worried about seeing Carol on Thanksgiving. It had seemed to him that when she saw him in more or less of a family situation rather than alone, as he usually saw her, she would see that he was just a kid and the difference between them would be evident.

He had been relieved it hadn't been like that. She might have watched the football game with the adults and eaten with the adults, but she had clearly been somewhere between the adults and the kids. He thought it was maybe because she wasn't married, but Mr. McClure wasn't married, and he had definitely been an adult. But then, teachers were always adults.

He had thought before of asking her to one of his football games. He wasn't one of the school stars, although it was possible he would be by his senior year, but he got to play part of every game, and he was a good player. And since she liked football so much, seeing him play might not be a bad idea.

There was only one home game left, and he decided to ask her if she wanted to come to it. He stopped by her place that Friday after practice, and when she asked him how practice went, which she always did, he said, "It's the last one. The season's over after tomorrow's game."

"What'll you do after school from now on?"

He shrugged. "Go out for basketball, I guess." It wasn't his best sport, but he liked it okay. If he thought he could get a job after school, he would have opted for that, but there just weren't any jobs around that weren't already taken.

She didn't say anything that would give him an opening, so finally he just asked outright, "Would you want to come see our game?"

"I'd love to."

He relaxed in his chair and took a long drink of the Coke. "Great. I guess you know where it is."

"I've driven by the high school."

"Great." He couldn't think of anything else to say.

"I haven't been to a football game in a long time."

"It's just high school; no big deal." Then, remembering, he added, "Dad told me your dad was a high-school football coach."

She nodded, for some reason acting as if that were a subject she didn't want to pursue. Maybe he'd said the wrong thing; maybe her dad was dead. "You never mention your folks," he said, taking a chance.

"I don't keep in touch with them. My brothers all played high-school football. One of them even played college, got an offer from the pros, but he didn't take it."

Willie couldn't imagine not taking an offer from the pros. That was one of the easiest ways he could think of to make a lot of money. "What'd he do instead?"

"He's a developer. Puts up shopping centers."

"That's probably what I'll do; some kind of construction work. If I can get it, anyway. Not much building going on around here."

"You going to stay in Rock Ridge all your life, Willie?"

"I guess."

"Why?"

Willie tried to think of an answer to that but couldn't. So he said, "I like it here," which he didn't figure was much of a reason.

"If you could be anything you wanted to be, Willie, what would you choose?"

"I guess I'd play for the pros. Your dad ever play for the pros?"

"No. He played college football at Illinois. He liked coaching, though. He coaches college out in California now."

"Your family's out in California?"

She shook her head. "Just my dad. My parents got a divorce when I was a kid."

"Like me," he said, not really wanting to talk about it and pretty sure he shouldn't have said anything, because now she looked upset.

"Your parents are divorced?"

"Yeah, I guess. My mom took off a few years ago; I haven't seen her since, but my dad has."

"My dad took off."

"Have you seen him since?"

She shook her head, and he thought maybe she was trying to hold tears back. Her mouth looked tight, the way his always got when he was trying not to cry. Not that he cried anymore, but when he was a kid, sometimes he did. "Did you love your dad a lot?"

She turned her face a little away from him just the way he did when he was afraid someone might see him break down, and he got up and took his Coke can over to the sink to give her a little time to get it together. He could tell she was just like him, that she'd rather die than let anyone see her cry. "It was okay," he told her, "about my mom taking off, I mean. She wasn't very easy to live with for a while there. She made things really bad for my dad."

He turned around, but she was still facing away from him. He figured he'd tell her a little about his mom; maybe that would make her feel better. He could bet her dad hadn't got strange, as his mom had. "She started reading the Bible all the time, really taking it seriously. She started thinking just about everything was a sin. Like—listen to this—like she thought laughing, just having a good time, was some kind of sin. Our house got real quiet for a while there."

"Did you feel like she deserted you?" she asked him, her voice sounding a little strange, but at least she was looking at him now, and he couldn't see any tears.

"Well, yeah—I mean, she did desert me, but it was my dad I felt sorry for. I don't know how it was with your dad, but with my mom it was kind of a relief not to have her there. She hadn't been like my mom at all for about a year."

"I guess that would make it easier," said Carol, looking as if she were remembering. "With me there was no warning. Just one day my dad wasn't there anymore, and we had to move in with my grandparents. And after that the only ones who would talk about him were my brothers, and pretty soon even they stopped."

"The thing about my mom was, she embarrassed us. I couldn't even have my friends over or anything, because she'd make them feel real uncomfortable and always want to lecture them from the Bible. I guess everybody around here knew about it."

Carol said, "I just really loved my dad. I thought he loved me; I thought I was his favorite."

"Yeah, I thought my mom loved me, too. At least my dad does, though, and you still had your mom."

"Yeah," said Carol, looking as if that wasn't any consolation. "So you haven't seen your mom since she left?"

He shook his head. "No. She's living in some kind of commune with a bunch of other people who are into the Bible; that kind of thing. My dad went out there a couple of times, but I didn't want to go. I used to think maybe she'd change, come back and be the way she was before."

"I used to think my dad would come back, too. Or perhaps I could go live with him."

"Dad says that kind of thinking isn't realistic, and I guess he's right."

"You get along with your dad?"

"Pretty good. The thing is, Mom used to be the strict one when I was little, and now I guess Dad thinks he has to be. It's okay, though; he's pretty fair."

He guessed Carol had had enough talk about parents, because she got up and showed him some of her new ideas for the Aunt Lolly cards. He could see they were pretty funny, and he smiled at them, but he couldn't really bring himself to laugh. And he hadn't even got Carol to smile that day.

CAROL FELT like a complete failure. For a long time she had wanted to get Willie to bring up the subject of his mother. She had had the notion that he was probably holding it all in and maybe needed someone to talk to, and she, of course, was going to be the understanding friend who could help him.

Instead, she had been the one who had got upset, the one who had the difficulty talking about her own father. In some ways Willie seemed more adult than she was. Well, Willie had his father to talk to about it, and she guessed that made the difference. At least she could see he wasn't really in any need of her help, that he had adjusted just fine.

She was happy that Willie had invited her to his game. She had thought of going to some of the other games but thought maybe it would cause talk if she went to see Willie play. For all she knew, his father might resent their friendship, or people might be talking about the fact that he spent a lot of time at her place. She wouldn't have thought a thing about it in New York, but she knew that small towns were different, that everyone talked about everyone else.

On Saturday, when she went over to get her car, Raney must have been watching for her, because he came right out of the house and said, "Willie says you're going to his game."

She nodded, hoping he wasn't going to make some remark about her going.

But he just said, "No sense in both of us driving. Why don't you get in the truck. I'll be right out."

She nodded again. It made sense, and it would probably look better if she was there with Willie's father.

She was sitting in the truck, shivering, when he came out, carrying a blanket over his arm and a thermos in his hand. She should have thought of that herself. It was colder out than she had expected, and the temperature seemed to be dropping. Her leather jacket kept the upper part of her warm, but her legs in the jeans were already cold, and she should've worn gloves.

"Willie's pleased you're going to see him," said Raney, starting up the truck and letting it warm up for a minute.

"I would've gone before if I'd known he wanted me there."

"Are you kidding? It'll make his day."

"He's a good kid."

Raney backed up the car, then pulled out on the road. "Yeah, he is. Sometimes too good. Once in a while I keep hoping he'll tear loose with me."

"What would you do if he did?"

"Whip the hell out of him!"

Startled, Carol turned to look at him and saw his grin. "You wouldn't really, would you?"

"No. Not that my daddy didn't do it to me on more than one occasion. I was always testing him, though; pushing him to the limits. I guess a lot of kids are like that, right?"

From the way he said that, she was sure Willie had told him about her own father. The last thing she wanted from Raney was sympathy, so she changed the subject. "It's getting pretty cold out."

"Supposed to go down into the twenties tonight. Might get a bad winter this year."

"That's cold enough for snow."

"Not forecasting snow."

She turned to look at him. "You mean it actually snows here?"

He gave a bark of laughter. "Course it snows, woman."

"I didn't think it snowed in the South."

"Well, you thought wrong. We might not get the snow you get up North, but it's for darn sure we get more in the mountains here than you get in New York City."

Carol didn't mind the thought of snow; in fact, she liked it. It's just that she hadn't anticipated it. "What about the roads? Do they keep them clear?"

"County does a pretty good job. Don't you worry none. Willie'll keep the driveway shoveled for you."

They were still talking about the possibilities of snow when Raney turned into the high-school parking lot. Judging by the cars and the people, it looked as though all of Rock Ridge turned out for the football games.

She followed him into the stands where they squeezed in between some people Raney apparently knew. If there had been more room, she would have moved away from Raney, for they were shoved up against each other pretty tightly. But she was shoved up just as tightly against the stranger to her right, and at least the two bodies were making her a little warmer.

Without even asking, Raney spread the blanket out across their laps so that it covered their legs, then opened the thermos and handed it to her.

"Coffee?" she asked.

"And a little something to keep out the cold."

She took a swallow and felt the warmth spread through her body. It tasted like more liquor than coffee, but she didn't mind. She passed it back to him and was relieved to see he only took a swallow before screwing on the top and putting it at his feet.

She had forgotten how much she enjoyed being out at a football game, any football game. In fact, it was good just being outdoors. Except for an occasional walk, she spent most of the time in her cabin.

Everyone got up to sing the national anthem and then went right into a rousing rendition of what must be the high-school cheer song. Raney was singing right along with the rest, and when they sat back down, she said, "Did you go to this high school?"

"Sure did. Even had the same football coach. We thought he was a pretty old guy at the time, but looking back at it, it must have been one of his first assignments. Doubt he was more than in his early twenties at the time.''

Carol had expected the game to be rough. She had had some idea that the kids, some of them big farm kids, would play a better game of football than her own high-school team had, but she was disappointed in that. They were fun to watch, but their level of expertise was more like junior high, if she remembered correctly. But then her own high-school team had been predominantly younger editions of Mean Joe Greene, and several of them had gone on to play pro ball. These boys all seemed to be like Willie; too nice to really get out there and kick the hell out of each other.

Willie was a linebacker and was put in a few times during the first half, but he didn't do anything spectacular; and the game wasn't too exciting when halftime came, with the score 3-0 in favor of the visiting team. Carol knew that if it weren't for the cold she would be feeling drowsy at that point, for she and Raney had finished off the thermos, and her head was feeling a little fuzzy.

She got up and stretched, spotted Donna Lee a couple of rows behind them and waved, then settled back down into the warmth provided by Raney and the man on her other side.

"You okay?" she asked him.

"Sure. Something the matter?"

"I'm just not used to drinking that much."

He gave her a closer look, then said, "Want me to try to get us some coffee?"

"Plain coffee?"

He chuckled. "That's all they sell here. I'll be back in a minute."

She made room for him to get by, then missed the warmth of his presence. He'd been nice to her during the game. Really nice. There was a little football talk, and he hadn't talked down to her at all, just acted as if she knew as much about it as he did, which she did. He had named the players for her, sometimes telling her things about their families. A couple of the boys on the team had fathers who had played on Raney's team when he had been in high school.

She wondered briefly what it would feel like to have that kind of continuity in a town but then decided it was something she would never know. Certainly Chicago no longer felt like home to her, nor did Evanston. She supposed New York was home, although there was something about the city that never gave off that kind of feeling.

And thinking of homes and hometowns and continuity was really just a method of getting her mind off what she was really thinking. Or really feeling. Which was a growing attraction for Raney Catlin despite the fact she knew it was just another case of being attracted to the wrong kind of man. Still, leaning up against him during the entire first half had stirred up feelings she couldn't entirely blame on the liquor she had consumed. It wasn't just the need of a man, either, because if that were the case, the man on the other side of her should be stirring up those same feelings.

Luckily for her, she was dead certain those same kinds of feelings weren't being felt by Raney.

RANEY WAS STANDING in the long line for coffee and thinking that Charlene would never have gone to a football game with him. Not even to see her son. Not even in the good days before she got religion. Charlene would have sent them off with hugs and said something like how football was for men, how she'd just stay home and do some cleaning up and have dinner ready for them when they got home.

And there was nothing wrong with that. Charlene kept a spotless house and cooked good, wholesome meals, and he'd rather watch the game with his buddies, anyway.

What surprised him was that Carol turned out to be just as good company as his buddies. She didn't scream or act silly or ask him dumb questions. She just sat there enjoying the game and understanding it and putting no pressure on him to act any differently than he'd normally act.

Another thing was, she looked good. He had never really noticed it before, but outdoors she looked real good. He had looked around at some of the other gals he knew, and while their makeup looked mighty good in a dimly lit bar, her clean, clear skin looked a lot more appealing to him in the sunlight. He'd just bet she'd look good in the morning, too. If there was anything he hated, it was seeing a woman's smudged makeup in the morning, and damn few of them thought to wash it off at night if they were going to be making love.

He liked the way her hair blew around in the wind, too. The rest of the ladies all had scarves tied over their hairdos so as not go get them mussed up. But then

Carol didn't even have a hairdo. She just had hair, ordinary hair. He decided he liked that.

Of course, he realized that consuming whiskey while being pressed up next to her for an hour and a half just might be clouding his thinking. And the fact that she was one of the few avaiable women around. He was beginning to think it didn't matter if she wasn't his type. Hell, she wasn't going to be there forever. Anyway, it might be kind of interesting to get to know a northerner. All the women he knew were just about alike, almost interchangeable. Everyone who met her seemed to like her, and Willie was downright crazy about her.

Maybe he'd see about taking her to the Voyager tonight. Only this time he'd get her to dance, not shoot pool. And if things felt right on the dance foor, who knew how the evening might end?

And to top it off, what was just icing on the cake was that she lived within walking distance of him. You couldn't get any more convenient than that.

When he got back with the coffee, she gave him a smile. The smile was a little different. It still lit up her face, but he could tell at the same time that it was a little blurry, that maybe he shouldn't have poured so much whiskey down her. If he hadn't, though, she'd be freezing by this time; the temperature felt as if it had dropped a good fifteen degrees.

He moved in close to her even though there was a little extra room on the other side of him. He didn't mind her keeping his side warm, but he didn't feature letting the guy sitting on the other side of him do the same.

"Thanks," she said. "It feels good just holding it in my hands."

He looked down and saw that her hands were red, as was her nose. He felt like taking off his own jacket, wrapping it around her, taking care of her, but he knew instinctively that she wouldn't let him do that. He could read "independence" written all over her. Instead, he handed her the blanket and said, "Here, wrap it around you, I don't need it," then took hold of her coffee so she had both hands free.

She took the blanket, all right, but she said, "If you change your mind, just let me know."

What he would've liked to do was wrap the blanket around both of them, but he knew that even if he attempted to do that, she'd figure he just wanted to grab a feel under the blanket. And the funny thing was, grabbing a feel was just about the last thing on his mind. He would much rather just put his arm around her and hold her close, but there was never any point trying to convince a woman of that. They always figured a guy was out for what he could get.

Maybe that was true in high school. He knew damn well that had been true in high school. But so few of the girls ever put out anything that most of the guys walked around in a perpetual state of frustration. He was pretty much past that these days, but a little warmth from a lady could be a nice thing.

"I'm afraid it's not too exciting," he said to her. "Not like a high-scoring game."

"I don't mind. I like watching good defense."

He did, too, but he didn't exactly consider what he was seeing good defense. It was more like lousy offense. They'd had a better team when he was a kid, but in those days they still flunked kids, and some of the players were a good twenty years old. Not like these kids.

He could be proud of Willie, anyway. He wasn't really talented; he would never make the pros or anything like that, but the kid was determined. Every time the coach sent him in, he did his best, and that was about all you could ask. The kid didn't have the killer instinct, and that wasn't something that could be taught.

He'd had it more. Not as much as some of the guys but a lot more than Willie. Willie had some of his mother in him. Not the crazy part—he didn't figure Willie to ever get weird on him—but Willie was more serious than he was. Charlene had been pretty serious. He could probably count on his hands the times he remembered her laughing.

It hadn't bothered him when he'd been dating her. In those days, if she'd laughed, it would've deflated his ego. He'd have been sure she was laughing at him. Anyway, all he'd cared about in those days was sex, and the only way he could get that with Charlene was to marry her. The thing of it was, she acted as if she wanted it just as much as he did, except once they were married, she lost all interest. She had never refused him outright, but she certainly didn't show much enthusiasm.

He was thinking too much about sex and too little about the game, and if he didn't watch it, he was going to scare Carol off before he even made a move.

WILLIE SPOTTED his dad and Carol in the stands during halftime. He tried to get their attention, but he saw his dad get up and move out into the aisle, and then he had to get to the locker room with the other guys.

When they returned to the field after halftime, he nudged his best friend, K.C., and pointed out Carol to him.

"Yeah?" said K.C. "Who's that? Some friend of your dad's?"

"She's the one I told you about, the artist who does those cards."

"Oh, that one," said K.C., clearly uninterested.

"You think she's good-looking?" Willie asked him, hoping for some confirmation of his own opinion.

K.C. shrugged. "She's old, you know? What do you want me to say?"

"I think she looks pretty young for thirty," said Willie.

"Yeah, she could pass for twenty-five. After twenty-five they all look the same; you know what I mean?"

Willie gave it up. Anyway, you had to really know Carol to appreciate her. K.C.—if they didn't have big boobs, he didn't even look at them twice. Willie didn't think he ever even looked at a girl's face.

He was really glad Carol had come out to the game. He figured he looked his absolute best in his football uniform. He was sorry he wasn't the quarterback out there making touchdown passes and really impressing her, but maybe she wasn't the type who was impressed by quarterbacks. Most of the girls were, but that was the only position most of the girls even semi understood.

"You got a thing for her?" K.C. was asking him.

"What?"

"That lady up there you pointed out to me. You haven't even been watching the action."

"No, come on—she's thirty years old."

"I seen the way you look at her. You got something going, Willie? Getting a little instruction?"

"Hey, she's not like that. She's really nice; we're friends."

"You can't be friends with them, Willie; they're different from us."

Willie didn't even bother arguing the point. K.C. had a bunch of older brothers who cheated on their wives and a mother who hung out in bars when his old man was on the road. K.C. just never was going to have a good opinion of women.

Not that his had been all that good until he met Carol.

Chapter Seven

"Feel like stopping in at the Voyager for a drink?" Raney asked her as they walked out to the parking lot together.

"What about Willie? Aren't you giving him a ride home?"

"It's the last game of the season, and they won. Willie'll be out celebrating with his buddies. I remember how it was. I only hope the kid who drives has sense enough not to get loaded; the cops'll be on the lookout for that kind of thing tonight."

"I think I need a little time to sober up, maybe get something to eat," said Carol. And also to take a hot shower and thaw out, she was thinking.

"I could eat. Want to stop and get something?"

"Only if we go to McDonald's," she said.

He looked down at her and grinned. "You like McDonald's?"

"Sometimes. The game kind of put me in the mood for it."

"Ordinarily, I'd say sure, I could go for a Big Mac myself, but the place'll be crawling with high-school kids after the game. Ever been to Smitty's?"

"I never heard of it."

"Just a diner; doesn't look like much. The truckers go there; they serve some good hot food."

"Sounds good," she told him. Anything sounded better at the moment than another TV dinner, particularly since she was chicken to leave on her electric heaters when she wasn't home and the cabin would probably be freezing.

She climbed up into the truck and hoped it had a heater in it. If it did, though, he didn't turn it on, and she didn't ask. She figured he was as cold as she was, and if he could stand it...

"I'm glad they won," said Carol.

"About time. They've lost more than they've won this year."

"Willie tells me he's going out for basketball, too. Is that team any better?"

"If anything, it's worse."

The diner turned out to be crowded, too, but at least it was warm inside, and Carol didn't mind. It didn't look like her idea of a diner, more like one of the smaller Greek coffee shops in New York. The decor was minimal to nonexistent, but the food she saw on the tables looked delicious. She saw a couple of people eating what looked like homemade stew that was tempting.

"What do you recommend?" she asked Raney when they were seated and she was handed one of the extensive menus. She figured in a place like that some of the stuff would be good and some not so good.

"Anything that looks good to you. A couple run the place, and she's a great cook."

He ordered a hamburger, and she ordered the stew, and then he changed his mind and said the stew sounded good to him, too.

She had caught him nodding to some of the people when they came in, and she said, "You probably know everyone in here."

"Just about."

"You don't talk to them or anything."

"What for? I see them all the time."

She thought of New York where it was a real occasion if you ran into anyone you knew. She had never lived in a place where you were always running into people you knew because you knew everyone. Something about it appealed to her, while at the same time she knew she wouldn't like losing her anonymity that completely.

"Have you ever been to New York?" she asked him.

"Never have. Guess you must like it up there or you wouldn't be living there."

"I like some things about it."

"What?"

He seemed genuinely interested, so she answered him honestly. "This might sound strange, but I always rather liked the sense of danger. Chicago had it, too, but Evanston was always quiet and nice and rather boring. I like street life. I like walking out and having all kinds of things happening around me. Cities make me feel really alive."

"Why'd you leave? Why come down here where hardly anything ever happens?"

"The sense of danger. The street life. They got to me after a while, and I wanted a change."

"You like living in J.J.'s cabin?"

"Very much. It feels small at times, and sometimes I start talking to myself out loud, but most of the time I love it. Do you know Mr. Rafferty well?"

"Everyone around here knows everyone else well. When I was a kid, I thought he was a little strange, being a writer and all, but once I moved where I am now, we got pretty friendly. We'd do a little fishing together, hunting. Real talker, but I always found him interesting."

"I've been reading his books."

Raney smiled. "J.J.'d be pleased to hear that. I read a couple of them; couldn't get too excited about them, though."

She must have looked surprised, because his smile broadened, and he said, "Didn't think I read, did you?"

"I hadn't really thought about it."

"I generally don't, but I was laid up in the hospital once and had nothing better to do. Nothing serious. Had a herniated disk, and the only way they could keep me immobile while it healed was to put me in a hospital bed. Insurance covered it."

The food came, and all conversation ceased as they started in on the stew. When their plates were clean, Raney said, "You eat as fast as I do."

She grinned. "That's because I grew up with brothers. If I didn't keep up with them, they stole my food."

"A southern boy wouldn't do that. He'd show his sister some respect."

"I didn't want respect; I wanted to be just like them."

He laughed. "That doesn't come as any news to me. In fact, I'm just waiting for the check to arrive, 'cause I have a feeling you're going to wrestle me for it."

"I certainly intend paying my portion."

"Look, I'll make a deal with you, darlin'. You let me get this one, and you can cook me dinner some night."

She felt herself warm at the "darlin'." No one had ever called her that before. "I'd be getting the best of the deal; all I ever cook are TV dinners."

"That the truth?"

She nodded.

"Okay, you win. You can pick up the tab, and I'll owe you a home-cooked meal."

"It's a deal," she told him. And she would much prefer seeing where Willie lived and eating with them than having to have a man over to dinner. "However, I'm not through yet. I think I'd like some apple pie."

Raney caught the waitress as she passed by and said, "We'd like some dessert, darlin'," and Carol thought, *So much for being called darlin'.* He seemed to call all the women that. Still, she liked the sound of it. Somehow, leaving the final g off darling made it sound much nicer, less phony than darling sounded.

They had apple pie with coffee, and then she saw Raney trying to look nonchalant while she paid the bill, but she could see it embarrassed him. Still, he let her do it, didn't even take the money from her and pretend he was paying it himself, and she gave him credit for that. She knew that the next day half of Rock Ridge would know the New York lady had paid for Raney's dinner.

She figured that was that. She had enjoyed the game with him and the dinner, and she was pretty sure he'd be heading down to the Voyager as soon as he dropped her off. Instead, he pulled up in front of the cabin and turned off the motor and the lights.

"What're you doing tonight?" he asked her.

"Probably watch a little TV."

"Mind if I watch with you?"

"You're not going to the Voyager?"

"I guess I could survive a night without the Voyager. If you'd rather be alone..."

She could swear he sounded wistful. Well, he probably didn't enjoy going home to an empty house, particularly after being married all those years.

"Come on in," she said, getting out of the truck and opening the door to the cabin.

She turned on the lights and found that indeed it was cold inside. She was turning on the floor heaters when Raney said, "Where're the logs? I'll build you a fire."

"I'm out of logs."

"Willie ought to know better than to let you run low."

She turned around and saw that he was angry. "It wasn't Willie's fault. I got the electric heaters and just haven't been building any fires."

"That's a damn fool thing to do, woman. Just what do you plan on doing when we get some snow and the power goes out?"

A chill went through her that had nothing to do with the lack of heat. "I hadn't thought about that."

"Happens all the time. Even in New York City, or so I've heard."

"I'm not helpless," she told him, thinking he was making too big a deal out of it. "I could always burn the furniture if I had to."

"Yeah? And how long do you think that would last you? I'll be over tomorrow and cut you some firewood."

She didn't like the way he was just assuming she was helpless. "I'll get Willie to do it; it'll give him a chance to earn a little money."

"I'll do it, and it won't cost you anything."

"Look, I'm not helpless, you know."

"I'm not saying you're helpless. I'm offering to do something I'd do for any neighbor."

They stared at each other for a few moments, and she saw he wasn't about to back down. It wasn't worth fighting over, so she finally went to the stove and put on some water to boil. "You play cards?" she asked him. She really didn't feel like watching television, and she thought it would be better to be across a table from him than next to him on the couch all evening.

"You still have poker in mind?"

"No. Not with two people. You play gin rummy?"

"Played it some. Get out the cards and we'll see how good you are."

Carol made them each a cup of coffee, then found her deck of cards and brought a pad and pencil to the table.

"Got anything stronger to drink?"

"No, I'm sorry. I've got Coke if you'd rather have it."

"Coffee's fine." He sat down across from her and started shuffling the cards. "Willie told me about those new cards you're doing. Mind if I see them?"

She got a few of the cards she had been working on and handed them to him.

He was smiling as he looked at them, nodding his head at a couple. "Aunt Lolly; I like that. I have a great-aunt Lizzie could've been this woman."

"You think they'll sell?"

"Around here they would. Willie's right; you're good."

"Thanks."

"Let's see if you're as good at cards."

It was a treat having someone play cards with her. She liked cards; she was good at them, but in New York no one ever seemed to play cards. But then in New York hardly anyone she knew ever stayed home at night.

They were pretty evenly matched. Raney was better at knowing what cards were out, which ones she picked up. She never bothered with that; it took too much concentration. When she won, it was usually because she changed her mind halfway into the hand about what she was going for, and that always managed to confuse the kind of opponent who kept track of cards.

He beat her by only a few points the first game, and she did the same on the second. Then it was two out of three, then three out of five, and she was disappointed when Raney finally conceded defeat and got up. She could've played all night.

She thought he was going to head home, but instead he went over and sat down on her couch. "Come on over here," he said.

She felt the slightest bit of apprehension. Not knowing what he had in mind, she stayed where she was.

"You got that scairt-rabbit look on your face again. I'm not going to bite you. It's just that those wooden chairs aren't all that comfortable, particularly after spending the afternoon sitting in those stands."

Feeling a little foolish, she got up and joined him on the couch. She lit a cigarette for something to do and was startled when he took the cigarette out of her hand and put it in an ashtray, then put his arm around her and drew her next to him.

"You said—" she began, feeling she was losing control of the situation.

He cut off her words with, "I said I wouldn't bite. The first time I bite you, you call me on it now, you hear?" And before she could say anything else, he put his other arm around her; she found her head against his chest, and he was resting his chin on her hair.

"Relax, darlin'. I don't have anything more in mind than a little snuggling; that's all. Sometimes I think you don't know the first thing about men."

Sometimes she had to agree with that. It certainly hadn't been snuggling she thought he had in mind. It felt okay, though, kind of nice. His flannel shirt was soft against her cheek, and he felt warm, reassuring.

"Tell me about your work," she said to him, afraid of the silence.

"No need to start a conversation," said Raney, one hand now smoothing the hair back from her face.

"It seemed like a good idea," she said, causing him to laugh.

"You think I can't read your mind? You're thinking you're alone in a cabin in the middle of nowhere with some questionable character who definitely outweighs you and you've left yourself open to any kind of attack—" He broke off at her laughter. "I'm wrong? That's not what you're thinking?"

"You'd be amazed at what I'm thinking," she said, amazing herself by even saying such a thing.

"Now you can't say something like that and then just shut up," he told her in a warning tone.

"I'm not afraid of you, Raney. At least not physically. I was just thinking it felt comfortable."

"Let's go back aways here. Not physically? How are you afraid of me?"

"I don't know what I meant by that."

"I figure you know exactly what you meant. In fact, you're one of the most careful speakers I ever met."

"You're the one starting a conversation now."

"You got something better in mind?"

"No," she said, a lie seeming imperative.

"Liar," he said, and she turned to look at him and deny it, or maybe she really had in mind what happened next. His mouth met hers in the most natural way, and she found that Raney Catlin was a very good kisser. His mouth was soft and moved around nice, and he didn't immediately try to ram his tongue down her throat. She liked leading up to things slowly, and Raney was taking his time and just feeling her out. In fact, it was so nice that she was afraid that whatever came next might be even nicer, and wanting to prolong that moment, she broke off the kiss and smiled at him.

He pulled her head back against his chest. "I figured by this point you'd be throwing me out of your cabin."

"I doubt that. I imagine you do pretty well with women."

"You're different."

"I don't know about different, but I never thought I was your type."

"You're not. But then you couldn't very well be my type if I've never known your type."

"I figure Donna Lee's your type," she said, meaning it, hoping he wouldn't think she was jealous.

"She is. She's like all the women I've known. Familiar. Just like your type's probably up there in New York."

"Not really."

"You don't like those New Yorkers?"

"You might not believe this, but you're more my type. It's just that I've never thought it was the right type for me."

"Maybe you've been wrong."

"I don't think so," she said, wishing they'd stop talking about it. She thought it was much too soon to be discussing types at all.

"Well, you might be familiar with my type, but I'm sure as hell not familiar with yours. What do you want me to do now, darlin', get up and go home?"

"What do you usually do?"

"Usually I know where I stand."

She moved out of his arms and could hear his sigh of disappointment. But instead of standing up, as she was sure he was expecting her to do, she knelt on the couch beside him so that her face was on a level with his. "I might be making a big mistake, Raney, but I don't want you to get up and go home."

"You sure of that?"

She nodded.

"Does this couch pull out?"

"Yes."

His smile revealed evil depths.

RANEY HADN'T KNOWN he could be so gentle with a woman. He also hadn't known how turned on he could get by a slim body. He was used to large breasts, the kind that spread out flat like pancakes when the woman was on her back, not the small, firm kind that looked good from all angles. He liked her slimness, too. Her body seemed all of a part, flowing together in smooth lines. No bulges where arm met chest or legs met torso. In fact, she looked better without clothes than with, which was a first in his experience.

He wasn't gentle with her because he thought she was fragile or because she seemed to demand it.

Something inside him seemed to take over, wanting him to be loving with her, caring, wanting it to be an experience neither of them would have cause to regret.

She didn't say a word while they made love, and he took her cue and kept silent, too, instead trying to convey to her with his eyes what he was feeling. And he was feeling a lot. In fact, he was feeling a hell of a lot more than he had counted on. But the thing was, he didn't mind. He found he would've hated going to bed with her and not caring.

When it was over—and it was over pretty quickly, because he found he was every bit as excited as a high-school boy—he held on to her, liking the way she fit in his arms, liking the smooth feel of her skin, her soft hair, the clean scent of her.

He felt this big urge to say something to her and put his feelings on the line. But something stopped him. Maybe the fact that she wasn't saying anything herself, maybe the thought that it might spoil something that was perfect. Instead, he tried to formulate in his mind just what he was feeling, and in about the middle of that he must've fallen asleep.

He opened his eyes to see her sitting up in the bed, shaking his shoulder. He smiled at her, thinking she was ready to try it again and knowing that he was.

"It's four in the morning, Raney," she said to him, as though he cared what time it was.

He reached up and ran the back of his hand along her cheek to feel the warmth. "Must've fallen asleep."

She gave him a rueful look. "We both did. Can I fix you some coffee or anything before you go?

She got off the bed now, a blanket wrapped around her. He sat up and said, "You throwing me out?"

"Don't you want to get home?"

"My god, darlin'—why would I want to get home?"

"What about Willie?"

"Willie's used to my staying out."

She hesitated, her eyes not meeting his. "But he'll know you were here."

Sure he'd know. He would've seen the truck parked outside. "What difference does it make?"

"I'd rather he didn't know."

"You care what he thinks?"

She nodded.

That really surprised him. "I wouldn't have figured you to care what anyone thought."

"Please don't take it personally, Raney, but I would rather you left."

"How can I not take it personally?"

She came back to the bed and sat down beside him, putting her face against his chest. "I'm not saying I don't want to see you again, Raney, if you still want to see me. I'd just rather you left now. Please?"

He put his arms around her, holding her tight for a moment, then gave her a slap on the bottom. "I won't hold it against you, darlin'. Never mind the coffee, though; no sense in drinking something that'll keep me up when I'm going straight to bed."

He got dressed quickly, and when he was at the door, she came into his arms again, and he hated the thought of leaving and going home to his cold bed. Still, it was her house, and he'd respect her wishes.

"I'll be over to chop that wood tomorrow," he told her, and she didn't give him an argument, just a smile that let him know she'd be glad to see him when he got there.

WILLIE LAY AWAKE in the darkness, waiting for the first sound of his father getting home. He had about given up hope he was coming home at all.

He had been in such a great mood. First winning the game and having Carol out there to see him. Then going out with his buddies, driving to the town thirty miles away where the opposing team was from, driving down the streets of the town, honking the horn, yelling out victory cheers.

K.C. had managed to buy them a six-pack of beer, which four of them had shared. They had been feeling no pain when the carful of kids from their rival school pulled up alongside them and started yelling out taunts. They had followed that car down a back road, ready for a fight, but it turned out the guys had a full six-pack in their car and were willing to share.

He knew he was getting home past his curfew but wasn't too worried about it, since he figured his dad would understand the celebrating. And if he didn't, if he got grounded for a few days, that wouldn't be anything new.

It hadn't even registered at first when they had driven past Carol's cabin and he had seen a truck parked outside. It registered fast enough when K.C. said, "Wasn't that your dad's Chevy back there?" He had felt instantly sober when just a moment before he'd been having trouble to stop laughing.

He got in the house and went to bed. It didn't even matter that he was getting away with breaking curfew. To hell with curfew; that was for kids, anyway. He lay in bed rationalizing what his dad could be doing over at Carol's.

Maybe they were just talking, getting to know each other. Maybe watching some late movie on TV. He knew that was about it as far as things to do in the cabin.

But when it reached two in the morning and then three and still his father hadn't got home, none of his rationalizing was doing a thing to untangle the knot in his stomach that had come from realizing, deep down, just what his father and Carol were really doing to pass the time. Not that he would have thought it of Carol; his father, though, he knew.

That he could picture them was the trouble. He'd seen movies about it at school; he had seen pictures in magazines some of his friends' fathers had at their houses. He had even read a book on the subject he had lifted from a drugstore, something about all the ways to make a woman happy.

Willie had never gone all the way with a girl himself, but he still knew the score. The most he had done so far was touch a few girls' chests outside their clothes and once, when Johnny Bagley's older cousin was visiting from Atlanta, see a girl stark naked. Her name had been Cindi, and she had liked taking her clothes off in front of boys, but there was no touching. Although Johnny said she had gotten in bed with him one night when they were all alone in the house and he had put his hand between her legs.

He figured his dad had more than his hand between Carol's legs, and the whole idea of it was making him sick. He knew his dad didn't even like Carol, had never said hardly a nice thing about her. He didn't really know about Carol. He couldn't remember her ever talking about his dad. Still, he didn't think that suddenly the two of them had fallen in love during the football game.

He figured his dad took advantage of Carol. He knew it wasn't anything like rape. He was sure his father wasn't capable of something like that. But he knew how Carol was. Carol was nice and polite and probably wouldn't want to make a scene. And his dad would've taken advantage of that. He felt like killing him. His dad knew Carol was his friend. Knew and still went right ahead and spoiled her forever.

He was so convinced by then that his dad would spend the whole night with Carol that at first he didn't hear the front door open and the familiar sounds of Raney coming home. Sober this time, and Willie couldn't figure out whether that was a plus or a minus.

He heard his father walking softly up the stairs and then approach his door. Trying to keep his voice sounding normal, Willie said, just matter-of-fact like, "How'd you like the game?"

At least his dad didn't turn the overhead light on and wouldn't see his face. "Good game, Willie—glad you won."

"Carol like it?"

"Sure she did. She really knows football. Said to tell you she was proud of you."

He just bet she said something like that. "You have a good time with her?"

A pause; then, he said, "Carol?"

"Yeah. I saw your truck over at her place when I got home. She your new woman, Dad?"

Another pause. "Little early for that, Willie."

"But you made it with her, right?"

"Let's just say we got along real fine."

He had to hear it, had to hear the words. "You sound like a kid making up excuses or something."

"And you sound like a parent, Willie. You know what happens between men and women; you don't need to ask me."

He heard him walk off then. But he had admitted it, hadn't he? Maybe not spelled it out but admitted it. He didn't think he could live with him anymore. How could he live with someone who was doing that to the person he loved?

It should've been a good day, a real good day. Instead, it was probably the worst day of his entire life.

Chapter Eight

For the first time that she could remember, Carol found herself wishing she weren't alone when she woke up on Sunday morning. She hugged the comforter to her for warmth, the chill air of the cabin keeping her from getting right up and putting water on to boil.

She might have let him spend the night if it hadn't been for Willie. Raney had been a revelation in bed. He had been warm and comforting and loving and hadn't tried to play any mind games with her after the sex. In fact, it hadn't been like a first time at all; it had seemed as though they were already familiar with each other's bodies, with each other's needs and desires. Right now it would be nice to be able to snuggle up next to him instead of having just the comforter for warmth.

She also knew for certain that he genuinely liked her and hadn't just been using her because he needed a woman. And what was surprising about that was that she knew he hadn't been any more attracted to her when they met than she had been to him. And yet, despite their different backgrounds, they had gradually grown to respect and like each other.

She was well aware they weren't a perfect match; in fact, far from it. Still, if the liking was there, the respect and, without a doubt, a physical attraction that could only grow after the experience of the night before, then it was enough to build on if they so desired, keeping in mind, of course, that nothing lasts forever and she would be back in New York in another few months.

She wasn't thinking marriage or permanency. It was not only far too soon for that; it was also unlikely. Still, it would be nice to have him around for the duration of her stay. It would even have been nice to have him around this morning, and she wished she could have let him stay.

She felt a little strange about the possibility of Willie finding out. For one thing, there had been no preparation. As far as Willie knew, she and Raney barely knew each other. She could only hope he would be pleased for his dad, but you never knew what kids' reactions were going to be.

Carol smiled as she remembered Raney's promise to cut wood for her today. At least she'd see him for a little while. She hoped he hadn't forgotten. But then, if he was feeling anything like she was, he would find some excuse to stop by. If he didn't, she would find some excuse to use her car. As far as that went, he owed her a home-cooked meal, and what better time than a Sunday night?

And if he did stop by, she wouldn't want him to catch her still in bed. She sat up and found her socks on the floor next to the bed, put them on, then headed for the bathroom to get her robe. She turned up the electric heaters to high, put water on to boil, then took a quick, hot shower.

She was still sitting at the kitchen table in her robe when the knock came at the door. She was sure it was Raney, and with a sense of anticipation that had something to do with the fact she was still in her robe, she hurried to the door and opened it, a smile already on her face.

The smile died at the first glimpse of Willie's face. If a healthy teenage boy could look haggard, Willie did. He looked as though he hadn't slept in a month, but Carol knew that couldn't be true, because she had seen him only yesterday, looking as if he owned the world.

"Can I come in?" he asked, dead serious, not even waiting for her reply before walking in.

"Want something to drink, Willie?" she asked, hoping she was reading the situation wrong.

He was standing there looking at her as though she had betrayed him, and she felt a chill even before he said, "I thought you liked me."

"I do like you." She didn't know why, but unaccountably she was feeling guilty.

His hands went into his pockets, and his eyes met hers briefly before looking away. "As far as I know, up until yesterday you didn't even like my dad."

"I didn't feel one way or another about him," she answered truthfully.

"But all of a sudden you like him a whole lot better than you like me."

"I don't like him better than I like you, Willie."

There was a long, uncomfortable silence while Willie stared at her. "If you don't like him better than me, does that mean you'll go to bed with me, too?"

"Willie—"

"How about right now? I mean, you're dressed for it, right?"

His tone was so spiteful she froze, hardly recognizing her friend. Knowing she was the adult in the situation, she forced herself to reach out and touch his arm, trying to smile and ease the tension. "Willie, why don't we talk about this?"

He moved away from the contact as though scorched. "Don't start talking to me like a mother, Carol."

She stood there helpless. "I wouldn't even know how to talk like a mother. I thought we were friends."

"I've liked you a hell of a lot longer than my dad has, if he even does. Did you need a man that bad? Did you?"

"You don't understand, Willie," she said, knowing it for a platitude even as she said it.

"I understand, all right. I understand that you say one thing and you do another." And then, completely taking her by surprise, he grabbed her in his arms and was bending his head down to hers.

She tried to get out of his grip but couldn't, then moved her face out of the reach of his mouth. "Please don't do this, Willie. You're going to wish you hadn't later."

Ignoring her words, he shoved her back against the door. The thought that he could easily overpower her entered her mind, but it wasn't fright she felt; it was shame. She felt in some way that she had betrayed him.

She stood still, afraid of what would come next. But as suddenly as he had moved in on her, he now stood back, his arms hanging loosely at his sides. They were both breathing heavily, but he recovered first.

"I don't even want to touch you," he said at last. "You make me sick. The both of you make me sick." He swept her aside with one arm, then went out the door, not even bothering to close it.

The cold air finally penetrated her consciousness and she moved to close the door and lock it. Wanting comfort when none was there, she went back to bed and crawled beneath the covers.

What a mess she had made of things. She had alienated Willie and ruined the possibility of any kind of relationship with Raney. She should have known how the boy felt about her. No, that wasn't being honest. She had known, or at least sensed it, but her way of dealing with it had been to ignore it, to pretend it wasn't there. Just as her way of dealing with the situation now would be to run right back to New York if she could. Only she couldn't. Not unless she wanted J. J. Rafferty for a roommate.

RANEY HADN'T GIVEN a thought to the questions Willie had asked him when he got home until his son came down for breakfast and refused to speak to him.

At first, Raney didn't even notice that Willie wasn't speaking to him, because Raney didn't like talking in the morning and he figured that for once the kid was being considerate. Finally, though, the silence began to feel so abnormal that Raney roused himself enough to say, "Get in some celebrating last night?"

He expected to be told about half of what had occurred, knowing that was what he would have told his own father. Instead, he was given an icy look of contempt, which was a totally new look in Willie's repertoire of looks.

"Little hung over?" he asked his son.

Willie held the contemptuous look for another few seconds, then looked down at the bowl of cereal in front of him. What also seemed unlike him was that he wasn't spooning it into his mouth.

"Somethin' bothering you, Willie?"

"Go to hell," muttered Willie.

Raney was halfway up from his chair. "What did you say, boy?"

Willie raised narrowed eyes to his. "You heard me. You can just go to hell. Both of you!"

Raney stifled an urge to reach around the table and grab the kid's arm and teach him just how to speak to his father. But it was unlike Willie to behave like this, and he was sure there must be a good reason. "What's the problem, son?"

"You had to try to take her away from me, didn't you? You just couldn't stand it that she liked me. Was it worth it? Was she good?"

"If you're talking about Carol, you better shut up your mouth," Raney told him. He'd be damned if he was going to let the kid bad-mouth Carol that way.

Willie smiled, a smile that was eerie in that his eyes were a blank. "Do you love her, Dad? You two going to get married?"

"You're talking foolish. Willie."

"You had to use her, didn't you? You didn't even like her, but you had to prove you could have her."

Raney could see the tears threatening his son; then, before he could say anything, the kid had knocked his cereal bowl over with his arm, then jumped up from the table and run from the room. Seconds later he heard the front door slam.

Now that he thought about it, it was something he should have foreseen. He had been aware that Willie had a crush on Carol; the kid talked about nothing else these days. Still, for some dumb reason, he had thought Willie would be pleased that he and Carol were now friends. Kind of one big happy family.

That had really been dumb thinking. It's just that he had never thought in terms of competing with his son or edging his son out or anything like that. And it wasn't as though the kid had a chance in hell of interesting a thirty-year-old woman in him. Still, it hadn't been the smartest move he ever made.

Well, one thing was for sure. The good mood he had got up with this morning had sure dissipated. He had figured he would stop by and see Carol later, maybe invite her back to the house for dinner. Yeah, what he'd had in mind was one happy family. Not that he was going to let some kid dictate what he could do and what he couldn't do. Hell, Willie just wasn't being realistic if he thought Carol was his. Carol was an adult with an adult's feelings.

Still, whoever said kids were realistic? He remembered having a crush on one of his teachers when he was a kid. You couldn't have convinced him at the time that anything wasn't possible.

It was housecleaning day, and he might as well get it over with. Willie kept the place picked up during the week, but on Sundays Raney always dusted a little and ran the vacuum around. Twice a year he hired in Emma to do some real cleaning, but the rest of the time they managed to keep it up pretty well.

While he worked, Raney tried to think of the conversation he would have with Willie when he returned. A real father-son talk. Not about sex, nothing like that; Willie had to know all about sex by this time. What he probably didn't know, though, was about the needs adults have. At Willie's age he had figured his parents were beyond those kinds of needs. He'd set him straight on that.

He'd say something like, "You know, Willie, you're daddy isn't so old that he doesn't desire to have a woman in his life."

The thing was, he could feature Willie coming back with, "I thought that was why you went to see Maybelle?"

And then he would try to explain the difference between the Maybelles of the world and the Carols, only he had already said he didn't love Carol and they weren't getting married, which might create a little problem. Not that it wouldn't be possible to love Carol; he was already having really good feelings about her. And she was definitely the kind of woman you married. It was just a little soon to be thinking of either, that was all. Hell, he hadn't even much liked her before last night.

The trouble was, at Willie's age you either were madly in love, or you were totally indifferent. Except for sex. At fifteen you usually went around just wanting sex in general. He began to think that talking to Willie wasn't going to get him anywhere.

Maybe Carol should talk to him. From what he heard, they talked just about all the time, anyway. Yeah, it would probably be better coming from her. Willie might accuse him of using Carol, but his own opinion of her was high. He had a good idea Willie would listen to Carol and respect whatever she had to say.

He got through the cleaning faster than usual, and instead of turning on the football game, he changed into a sweater and some clean jeans and decided to take a walk down to Carol's to see how she was doing. He wouldn't take the truck in case Willie spotted it outside her cabin again. Might as well get it straightened out about Willie before he made any more trouble between them.

As soon as Carol opened the door, Raney could tell that Willie had already been by to see her. She looked even paler than usual and didn't seem eager to ask him in. He could hear the football game on in the background, and he said, "Is that the Redskin game?"

She nodded. "But don't ask me the score, as I haven't been able to concentrate. You better come in, Raney."

He spent a little time taking off his jacket and hanging it on the peg, then sat down on the couch beside her. "I guess Willie's been by."

She nodded, avoiding his eyes.

"Better tell me about it."

She seemed to hesitate, then poured it all out. When it came to the part where Willie pushed her up against the door, Raney let out a groan and shook his head. "He didn't hurt you any, did he?"

"No. He wouldn't do that."

Raney expelled a long breath. He told her about coming home that morning and about the scene at the breakfast table. "I guess I've made a mess of it," he ended up with.

"Not you. Me. I feel like I've betrayed him."

"Hell, Carol, he's only a kid."

Carol gave him a long look. "I remember what it's like being fifteen. Don't you?"

"Yeah, guess I do at that. I called it a crush he had on you, but in those days it never felt like a crush."

Carol nodded. "Kids can love just the same as adults. Maybe better."

Raney, who couldn't remember as an adult ever feeling the mindless passion he had felt at seventeen, had to agree. "Okay, so the kid thinks he loves you. What's the solution?"

"I don't think there is one. I don't see him forgiving either of us for this. I really feel terrible about this,

Raney. Guilty, too. He was my friend. Certainly my best friend in Rock Ridge.''

"Maybe you can use the past tense, but he's still my son. And I tell you, Carol, I can't let him control the situation. He's going to have to understand about us, that's all.''

"I think he understands perfectly.''

Raney knew that if he was a gentleman he'd say, "No, he doesn't understand. I love you, and that makes it all right.'' Except he valued the truth even more than he valued being a gentleman, and anyway, he didn't think for a minute that she'd believe it. "What do you suggest we do?'' he asked, hoping she wouldn't insist on cooling it for a while. They could be careful, maybe see each other where Willie wouldn't know about it.

But she said, "I suggest we apologize to him and try, if it's even remotely possible, to go back where we were before.''

"We can't let him run our lives for us.''

"I'm sorry, Raney, but I've never felt having an affair was worth ruining a friendship over.''

Affair. That was a New York word if he ever heard one. Still and all, the word he would have used wasn't much better. "And if the friendship's already ruined?''

She didn't say anything, just sat there wearing the most dejected face he had ever seen.

He put an arm around her, felt her stiffen, but pulled her over against him, anyway. "I had thought last night was just the start; I hadn't figured on it being the finish.''

"I know. I felt the same way."

"Don't we deserve it?"

She pulled away from him. "No. Not at Willie's expense. It's not as though we were in love or anything, Raney."

"Yeah."

"I think you'd better go. I think you ought to be there when he gets home. If you're not, he's going to assume you're over here, and jealousy can be really hard on someone, you know?"

He forced a smile as he got up. "Who knows, maybe we're exaggerating things. Everything might blow over in a day or two; you never know." But he could tell by her face that she no more believed that than he did.

WILLIE HAD RUN out of the house with the intention of never returning. Thoughts of running away, just disappearing, had come to him. They'd be really sorry if that happened, if he just vanished. They'd really feel guilty about that. Or maybe worse; maybe he'd get killed.

As he approached Carol's cabin, though, he had decided to confront her. Maybe it was all a lie, something his dad had made up to make himself sound big with women. Maybe Carol was perfectly innocent and he could just move in with her, punish his father that way.

But as soon as he got in Carol's cabin, he could sense her guilt. Still, he had to hear it, had to know she was as guilty as his father.

When he left her cabin, he was too upset to even plan a runaway. Plus he was dead broke, and hitch-hiking somewhere and then living in the streets didn't appeal to him a whole lot. He thought of his mother, then instantly rejected the idea of trying to find her. He wasn't a little kid having to run to his mother with his problems. His grandparents were a possibility, but they were over a hundred miles away.

Instead, he walked to K.C.'s house, hoping his friend would be at home. He was watching the game on TV, but when he saw the look Willie directed at him when K.C. asked if he wanted to watch the game, he quickly took Willie upstairs to his room and asked him what was the matter.

Willie told him about Carol and his father.

"So what's the big deal, Willie? I mean, it never bothered you before when your old man had girlfriends."

"I told you, K.C., she was my friend."

"Yeah? So what?"

"Listen, she admitted that she liked me better than my father."

"What's that got to do with sex?"

"Well, why not with me?"

K.C.'s eyes widened, and a grin split his face. "Be serious, Willie, will ya? First of all, with you it'd be illegal. I mean, the woman's not stupid, is she?"

"I wouldn't've told on her."

"You're my friend and all, Willie, and I appreciate your better qualities, but I gotta tell you, you ain't ex-actly a sex symbol. I mean not to an older lady. You know what I mean?"

"I didn't think she was like that."

"Like what? Human? You want to know something, Willie? My folks still have sex; I swear to God."

"Yeah, well, I could've figured that out, K.C. I mean your little brother, what is he, about three?"

"Okay, okay, but what I mean is, she probably felt like having a sex life, you know?"

"Then why did she move down here?"

"She's having one, isn't she? Oh, hey, Willie, I was only kidding. Listen, did you ever put the move on her?"

"I respected her."

"Yeah, well, your dad was a little smarter than you in that respect. Sometimes you gotta be assertive; you know what I mean?"

"It's too late for any of that, anyway, K.C. What I'm really wondering is, could I live here with you?"

"You nuts or something? You want to live in a house with seven kids when you got that big place all to yourself?"

"I don't feel like I can live in the same house with my father anymore."

K.C. looked around his room. "If you don't mind sleeping on the floor, I got a sleeping bag you could use."

"I don't mind. Would it be okay with your folks?"

"I think they'd want to talk to your old man, square it and all. You'd have to go home and get some clothes, anyway, right?"

Willie nodded. "Would you go with me?"

"Wait till the game's over and I'll get my dad to drive us. Listen, you eaten?"

Willie shook his head.

"Come on—I'll fix you a sandwich. And listen, don't pay no attention to my sister Francie. She's got a crush on you, but I guess you know that. She's going to think some miracle occurred when she finds out you're moving in here."

But Willie wasn't even listening. He was still picturing the look on Carol's face when he had pressed her against the door. He hated the thought that he had scared her; he had never meant to do that.

Chapter Nine

Carol was lonely for the first time. She found there was a difference between solitude, which she enjoyed, and being lonely for someone in particular.

She missed both Willie and Raney. Willie's after-school visits had become an anticipated part of each day, a time to stop work and relax and talk about all sorts of things.

As for Raney, she found it strange that she could miss someone so much whom she had seen so seldom. But the memory of their one night together didn't die; instead, she found her mind elaborating on it, constructing conversations and happenings that hadn't even occurred, but which might have occurred. In her imagination they had now had several nights together, and they began to seem real.

That week she left the cabin only once. The first snow had fallen, only a couple of inches, but the sight of it made her feel like a child, and she went outdoors and tramped through the woods for an hour, then returned and threw a few snowballs before once more locking herself inside. Still feeling guilty, she was afraid of running into Willie when she went to get her car, so she stayed at home and watched more television than she cared to watch and gradually depleted her supply of canned goods.

The weekend was particularly difficult. She knew that Raney and Willie were right down the road from her, yet they might as well have been a thousand miles away, so inaccessible did they seem. She found herself leaving her TV set on all the time just to hear the sound of voices in the background, something she had never done before.

A trip to the Voyager seemed a pleasure all out of proportion to what it had been in the past. Even a trip to the store took on an aspect of adventure in her mind. More than once she thought of returning to New York, but each time she told herself to give it a few weeks and see what happened. She didn't want to think of herself as someone who ran away from situations.

Finally, on a Monday morning, when she knew Raney would be at work and Willie in school, she braved the walk down to get her car. There was still snow on the ground, but the area in front of the garage was smooth and undisturbed. She wondered if Raney had found it strange that she hadn't been by for her car and how soon he would notice the tracks she was leaving.

She felt like a trespasser when she got her car out. She decided it was ridiculous to feel guilty over getting her own car and decided to leave it parked in front of her cabin for the time being. Despite the rent she paid, she no longer felt comfortable parking her car in their garage.

Feeling as if she had been sprung from prison, she drove the hundred miles to the nearest city and spent hours going from store to store. She stocked up on food and cigarettes, on art supplies, on magazines and paperbacks, and when she saw that the stores were decorated for Christmas, she also bought a tree stand and lights and a cassette with Christmas music.

She hadn't even thought about Christmas, but now she realized it was only three weeks away. Usually, by this time she had made her own Christmas cards and was mailing them out. She would have to work hard now to get them done in time.

She heard more snow predicted on the radio as she drove home. She liked the idea of a white Christmas, the kind she remembered as a child. Since being in New York, she could only recall one Christmas where they had snow that early in the year, and then by the actual day it had mostly melted, and the only place it was still visible was in Central Park.

It took her several trips to unload her car; then she treated herself to hot chocolate with marshmallows while she put her purchases away. After that she put Willie Nelson's tape on and listened to him singing Christmas carols while she sat at her drawing table and sketched ideas for a Christmas card.

She finally decided to go with a sketch of her cabin with a wreath on the door and snow on the ground. She didn't exchange cards with very many people. She sent them to her brothers, her agent and a few New York friends. She thought she might send one to Donna Lee, too. Maybe Raney and Willie, but she doubted it. That would be rather like beating a dead horse.

RANEY COULDN'T REMEMBER ever having been in such a bad mood for such a long stretch. He was a bear with the guys at work, curt with the businesses he delivered to and hurried home every evening to see if Willie maybe had changed his mind and moved back home. By Friday night he still hadn't, and Raney decided to really tie one on.

He spotted Donna Lee as soon as he entered the Voyager and headed over to take the stool next to her. He needed to talk to someone, needed advice, and Donna Lee, with three kids of her own, was elected.

"How have you been, Raney?" she asked him as soon as he sat down.

"Not so hot, Donna Lee."

She gave him the once-over. "Where's Carol? I figured, seeing you two together at the game and all—"

"Can I ask your advice?" he said.

"Ask away."

He told her about the situation, realizing as he did so that it wasn't advice he was asking for exactly; it was more like getting the whole thing off his chest. He didn't tell her the part about the sex. He didn't want her getting the idea he was the kind who talked afterward just in case he and Donna Lee ever got it on together. He made it pretty clear, though, that it hadn't just been a necking party.

"I hadn't heard about Willie moving out," she said, looking as if she couldn't understand how that bit of gossip hadn't made the rounds. "You got a real problem there, Raney."

"Damn right. And I can't see any way clear to resolving it."

"You want my advice?"

"That's why I told you, Donna Lee."

"What I think, Raney, is that you can't let your kids run your life for you. I mean you owe 'em some responsibility, that kind of thing. But when it comes to a personal life, you got to go with your own feelings."

"And I agree with you, darlin'; the thing is, Carol doesn't. She feels she's betrayed Willie."

"You seeing her at all, Raney?"

He shook his head. "No. As far as she's concerned, it's all over."

Donna Lee signaled the bartender for another beer, then turned back to Raney. "Well, look at it this way: it's not as though you were planning on settling down with her. Were you?"

"Once, Donna Lee. We were together once."

Donna Lee was nodding. "Right. That's what I mean. Now if you was in love with her, Raney, maybe I'd be feeling real sorry for you. But as it is..." She gave a shrug.

"Love. That's all you gals ever think about."

"It's something maybe you men ought to think about more often."

"I don't know, Donna Lee. I'm not even sure what love is. I figured I loved Charlene, but looking back on it, I married her for only one reason. How do you tell love from plain hormones?"

Donna Lee was smiling. "Yeah, I remember Charlene in high school all right. What was it you guys called her? Wasn't it the walker?"

Raney remembered all too well. "Yeah, on account of she walked home from more dates than any girl we ever heard of. You'd be parking with her somewhere after a date, and when push came to shove, out the door she'd go. Acted like whatever she had was made of 14-karat gold."

Donna Lee gave a snort of laughter. "Yeah. That's what we all thought love was in those days. I guess me and Glenn lucked out. After the passion sort of died down, we found we really loved each other."

"Doesn't always work out that way," said Raney.

"You're older now, Raney, and should've learned something along the way. Was it just hormones with Carol?"

He felt like telling her it was none of her business, but then again he had made it her business. "I like her; she's different. I've never known a woman like her before."

"Yeah, she is different," said Donna Lee.

"Intelligent, you know? Talented, too. I admire the way she can draw things like that."

"I guess you probably admire her pool shooting, too."

He looked over to see if she was making fun of him but couldn't detect any humor in her expression. "Yeah. First time I ever had that in common with a woman. Likes football, too."

Donna Lee took out a cigarette and leaned over for a light. "Looks like you two are a good match, Raney. Be a darn shame if you couldn't work things out. Want I should talk to her?"

"I couldn't ask that of you, Donna Lee."

"I'm offering."

"I guess it's worth a try; damned if I know what to do."

"What about Willie? You going to allow him to live over at K.C.'s house indefinitely?"

"I'm not going to beg him to come home."

"You men can be so stubborn."

"It's a matter of pride, Donna Lee."

"Nope. Stubborn's the correct word."

CAROL WAS SURPRISED by the knock on the door Monday morning. She had been waking up early lately and was at work when the interruption came. Thinking it might be the sample dolls Phyllis was sending down to her, she was expecting to see the UPS man at the door. Instead, it was Donna Lee.

"Come on in," said Carol. "It's good to see you."

Donna Lee, her face red from the cold, stepped inside and looked around. "This is real cute in here. I wouldn't mind a place like this all to myself."

"It's perfect for one person."

Carol took Donna Lee's coat, then asked her if she'd like some coffee.

"I'm disturbing you, aren't I?'

"I welcome disturbances, Donna Lee. Anyway, it's about time I took a break."

Donna Lee walked over to the drawing board and looked at Carol's work while Carol put some water on to boil. "How about hot chocolate with marshmallows? I'm becoming addicted to it."

"Low calorie hot chocolate?"

Carol laughed. "Of course."

"Sounds good to me."

They were sitting at the table drinking cocoa and smoking before Donna Lee brought up the subject of her visit. "I was talking to Raney down at the Voyager the other night."

Carol couldn't think of anything to say to that. Anyway, she had supposed the story had got around.

"What I told him," said Donna Lee, "and I'm going to tell you the same thing, is that you can't let your kids dictate your life. Now take me, for instance. One of these days I'm going to start seeing men again, and when that happens, you can bet I'm going to get all kinds of trouble from my kids. They get jealous, you know; they want you all to themselves. But I'm not going to let that stop me, and Raney oughtn't to, either."

"Willie's not my child; he was my friend."

"But that's the thing, Carol—he's a child."

"Did you feel like a child at fifteen?"

She could swear Donna Lee was blushing. "Hell, no, of course I didn't. And I could see Thanksgiving the kid had a crush on you. Followed you everywhere with those big eyes of his. Still and all, I'm assuming you don't feel the same way about him."

Carol almost choked on the hot chocolate. "No, of course not."

"It's not unheard of, you know."

"I don't know how I can convince you of this, Donna Lee, but he never, not even for a second, appealed to me that way. I guess I should've been aware how he was feeling, but I really thought we were friends."

"I believe you, honey. Raney said Willie got a little forceful with you."

Carol sighed. "It was a bad situation. He made me admit I liked him better than his father, and he knew very well what Raney and I had done."

"You like him better than Raney?"

"I know him better; we've been friends ever since I moved down here. Anyway, the way I like Raney is completely different from the way I like Willie. I didn't even like Raney for a long time. And I'll tell you, Donna Lee, it wasn't worth this happening."

"Raney's feeling real bad about it. You knew Willie moved out, didn't you?"

"No. I didn't know that."

"In with his friend K.C.'s family. Good people and all, but it's tearing Raney up. That and not seeing you."

"I doubt whether not seeing me is tearing Raney up."

"He's a good man, Carol. I think he has real feelings for you; probably more than he even knows."

"I have some real feelings for him, too. But the bottom line is, one night together isn't worth breaking up a family over. I'd give anything if I could just go back and have it all to do over again."

"That kind of thinking gets you nowhere, honey. Listen, Willie will come around eventually. With Raney, I mean. Those two was always close. I don't think even something like this is going to keep them apart for long. As for you and Raney, why don't you come on down to the Voyager? You could always see each other without Willie finding out about it."

Carol didn't see how that would be possible when the whole town knew what everybody was doing. Anyway, that was no solution. "I'm not sneaking around to see him, Donna Lee. I'm not going to be responsible for causing Willie any more unhappiness. It's just not worth it."

"What about Delbert?"

"Who?"

"You know, the art teacher. You heard from him?"

Carol shook her head. "He was supposed to send a message with Willie about my talking to his class. I guess that's out now."

"Why don't I give him a call."

Carol couldn't stop the smile. "Very subtle, Donna Lee. Raney's out, so now you're going to go with Delbert again."

"It's not natural spending all your time alone in this cabin. People are going to start suspecting you're a hermit."

"Call him; I don't care. I wouldn't mind talking to his classes."

"He wouldn't be bad for a friend, either."

"You're not bad yourself," Carol told her.

"What're you doing for Christmas, honey? Going home?"

"I'm staying here."

"You're welcome at my place for dinner. Be a raft a people again, but you know most of them now." Then, as though sensing Carol's thoughts, she said, "Raney won't be there. Goes to his folks for Christmas."

Carol thought of spending Christmas alone in the cabin and said, "Thanks, I'll probably take you up on the invitation."

Donna Lee stood up. "Gotta go. My little one gets home from kindergarten soon. But listen to me, honey. Anytime you feel like talking, you know where I live. Don't be a stranger, hear?"

THE WHOLE POINT of moving out of the house had been to punish his dad, but the problem was, for all Willie knew, his dad and Carol might still be seeing each other and be glad he moved out. The thought of that bothered him a lot.

At first, he enjoyed living at K.C.'s house. It was a lot different from living with his dad, having all those people around. The TV was always on, plus a couple of radios and a stereo, and K.C. had a bunch of video games they were allowed to play as much as they wanted. K.C.'s mom was a good cook, too, and there was always plenty of soda in the refrigerator and stuff like potato chips and popcorn. At first it was kind of like a holiday.

Then K.C.'s sister Francie started bugging him. She was only thirteen, still in junior high, but whenever he saw her around the house, she was wearing this dark lipstick and rolling her tongue out over her lips as if she thought she was sexy. It would've made him laugh if he had felt like laughing at the moment.

Plus, twice her mother had had to yell at her to put a robe on over her pajamas when she came to the breakfast table. K.C. told him that was on his account, that when just the family was there, pajamas were okay. Willie figured next she was going to do something gross like walk in on him when he was in the shower. The whole thing was making him nervous.

Thirteen. Did she really think he went for thirteen-year-olds? Maybe Carol was too old for him, but thirteen was for sure too young. What would you talk about with a kid that age, anyway?

He found he wasn't able to get to sleep very easily anymore. He wasn't doing too well in school, either. His dad always made him do his homework after dinner, but here no one seemed to care whether he did it or not, so he usually didn't. What difference did it make, anyway? Hell, in another year he could legally quit school if he wanted to. Quitting school was beginning to sound like a good idea to him. He could move away, get a job, have his own place. No one to tell him what to do anymore. Maybe by then he'd forgive Carol and she'd come and live with him.

Yeah, and maybe cows would grow feathers, too.

Mostly, though, he wanted to know what was happening at home. His worst nightmare was that Carol had moved in with his dad, that the two of them were now enjoying the place all to themselves and had totally forgotten about him.

He lasted it out at K.C.'s for ten days. Then he told K.C. he wanted to go home.

"Yeah, it's not exactly first-class accommodations here," observed K.C.

"It hasn't been bad; I just feel like my dad's getting off too easy. I'm going to go home and make life miserable for him."

"Revenge. Yeah, I see what you mean."

"You don't think that's rotten of me?"

K.C. grinned. "Sure it's rotten. It still has a lot of appeal, though."

"You think your dad would drive me over tonight?"

"Sure. Listen, though, Willie. You're going to break Francie's heart, you know."

"She's really beginning to bug me."

"Yeah, I noticed. I don't understand why she goes for you, actually. She got half the eighth-grade boys after her."

"She's a cute girl; I got nothing against her. She's just a little young."

"Well, she's not thirty; that's for sure."

Willie decided to change the subject.

CAROL WAS JUST GETTING OUT of her car with a load of groceries when Delbert pulled up. He got out of his car and hurried over to her, insisting on **relie**ving her of the bag of groceries.

"How've you been?" she asked him, thinking Donna Lee had moved fast.

"I hadn't forgotten about inviting you to speak to my classes," he said, waiting for her to unlock the door, then preceding her into the cabin. "This is cozy," he said, looking around. "You look like you're settled in."

"How about a cup of coffee, Delbert?"

"Fine. Or tea, if you have it."

Tea sounded good to Carol. She'd been consuming far too many marshmallows lately with all the hot chocolate she had been drinking.

Like everyone else who had been to the cabin, Delbert headed right over to her drawing table to take a look, giving Carol a chance to put away the groceries.

"These are very clever," he said, looking through a stack of cards she had completed. "My students are going to enjoy this. You will still come, won't you?"

"I'd love to," she replied, thinking she would have jumped at any opportunity to get out for a change.

"It's not that I have many students with a talent for art. There're a couple—you always get a couple. It's just that what you're doing is something I don't think would have occurred to any of them. As a possible job, I mean. I try to open their horizons, but it's an uphill job."

Carol remembered some of the things she had talked about with Willie and nodded her head. "Do many of them go on to college?"

"A few. The trouble is, it's never the kids you think would really benefit from college. Most of them just get jobs and get married. Only now there aren't even enough jobs."

"You grew up here, didn't you?"

"Yes. And I did get to college and could've got out, but I thought I could do more by coming back here and trying to help others to get out."

"I don't know," said Carol, fixing the tea. "Rock Ridge doesn't seem like a bad place to live."

"It's not; don't get me wrong. It's just that there really aren't any job opportunities. It should be the kind of place people retire to. For someone young there just aren't many options. I would think someone like you would miss all the cultural advantages of New York.

Carol gave him a sheepish look. "I'm afraid I'm not that big on culture. Oh, I enjoyed all the art around, but the rest of it was wasted on me."

"I was sure you'd be one of those sophisticated New Yorkers."

Carol laughed. "Maybe I am, at least compared to Rock Ridge. But sophisticated doesn't necessarily mean cultured. Actually, I'm probably more street smart than sophisticated."

"Next you're going to tell me you hung around in pool halls," he said, a teasing note in his voice.

Carol grinned at him. "No, that was purely my upbringing. My dad treated me like one of the boys."

They began to make plans about her visit to his classes, and while he went on about his curriculum and the different students, she found herself hoping that all of this wasn't going to lead to his asking her out. She liked him, all right—she still wouldn't mind having him for a friend—but she could tell after just a few minutes that she was never going to be physically attracted to him, while at the same time she was awfully afraid he was finding her attractive.

And even if she did find him physically attractive, she wouldn't be about to have a second affair in such a small place within such a short period of time. She figured that one man in the town would be okay; two might give her the title of town slut. She had instigated enough talk, she was sure, without giving cause for more gossip.

He did ask her out before he left, but it was such an innocent kind of date she didn't see how she could refuse. Surely going to the school play with one of the teachers wouldn't alarm anyone unduly. And she would insist on taking her own car and meeting him at the school.

"I'll see you next week, then," he said to her before leaving, alluding to the day she was visiting his class, not to the play, which was two weeks off.

"Thanks, I think it'll be fun," she told him.

"For me, too. I won't have to teach at all, just sit back and enjoy your lecture."

She stood at the window and watched him drive off, wondering at the vagaries of attraction. Why one man should attract her any more than another, she didn't know; all she knew was that if it had been Raney sitting across from her at the table, she would have been feeling a whole lot different.

RANEY WAS DOING UP the dinner dishes when Willie returned that night. The water was running in the sink, and he hadn't heard the front door open, but he heard it slam and stood motionless for a minute.

He suddenly felt shy about seeing Willie. He didn't know whether to go out and welcome him home or act as though nothing had happened between them. He finally decided to stay where he was and take his cue from Willie. But God, he was sure glad the boy had come home. The house had been too damn quiet and lonely without him.

When Willie didn't appear right away, Raney finished up the dishes, even found himself drying them when usually he just left them in the drainer to dry. When he had finished all he could possibly do in the kitchen, he got himself a beer out of the refrigerator, then turned off the light and went into the living room. He saw that Willie wasn't there at the same time he heard footsteps overhead.

He guessed the kid was upstairs unpacking, getting settled in. Raney turned on the TV, not even paying any attention to what came on, then sat down in his recliner and waited for Willie to appear. He'd be sincere with the boy, tell him how sorry he was for misunderstanding, for upsetting him. And then, if possible, get Willie's blessing to see Carol again.

He couldn't seem to get Carol out of his mind. Despite the fact that he spent a lot of time worrying about Willie, he found himself spending a lot of time thinking about her, too. Donna Lee didn't even look good to him anymore. Oh, she was a fine woman and a good friend, but he could no longer remember why he had ever been attracted to her. Conversely, he couldn't figure out why he hadn't been attracted to Carol sooner.

When an hour had passed and Willie still hadn't come downstairs, Raney found himself wishing he had welcomed the boy back as soon as he had come into the house. Now he felt a little strange about going upstairs, as though maybe he was too late. The kid might be feeling rejected and think he was ignoring him for some reason.

Something kept Raney glued to his chair. It couldn't be fear, he told himself. No reason for a man to be afraid of his own son. He guessed maybe what it was, was apprehension. Nothing had been resolved between them, and he didn't know where he stood with Willie.

Finally, at ten o'clock, Raney turned out the downstairs lights and headed upstairs. It was a little early to be turning in; usually, he waited up to see the news, but he didn't think he ought to wait any longer. Willie might be going to bed early, and he didn't want to leave it until morning.

Willie's door, which was usually left open, was closed. Raney could see a light on underneath, though, so he knocked and waited to be invited in. When no response came, he knocked again, then, feeling worried at the lack of reply, he opened the door and looked inside.

Willie was propped up in bed with a school book in front of him. He didn't look up at all, just continued staring at the pages.

"Glad to see you home, son," said Raney, his voice sounding a little funny to his own ears. He cleared his throat and tried again. "Been getting along okay?"

Willie looked up then, but his eyes looked cold and unseeing. He stared at Raney for a good minute, then lowered his eyes again to his book.

Feeling summarily dismissed, Raney pulled the door closed and stood outside in the hall for a minute. So that's the way it was going to be. He was home, but all was not forgiven. Well, Raney guessed that it would take a little time, but at least it was a start. At least they were together in the same house again.

But it sure wasn't anything to cheer about.

Chapter Ten

It happened on a Saturday. Raney drove into Bubba's station to fill up on gas, something he did a couple of times a week. He pulled into the self-service lane, turned off the engine and got out of his truck. He pulled the lever, took out the gas pump and had it inserted in his gas tank before he looked up. Then he wondered why he hadn't noticed it before.

There, in the full-service lane, was Carol's Mercedes. She was looking out the window right at him, and he felt as if the sun had come out and the temperature had lifted by a good ten degrees. Just her looking at him did that; she hadn't even smiled.

He was afraid she would pull out before he finished filling his tank, so he shut it off and left it at only a quarter full. Then, not hurrying, he walked over to her car and leaned down at her window. The window lowered, and she was just inches from him.

"How are you, Carol?" he asked, trying to find any differences in her and seeing none.

A smile briefly flickered on her face; then she was solemn again, her large dark eyes looking up into his. "I heard about Willie moving out."

"He's back now."

Now the smile did come, but it was a smile of relief, not a happy one. "I'm so glad, Raney."

He gave a shrug. "He's back, but he doesn't talk to me. Treats me like I'm invisible."

She looked down at her hands gripping the steering wheel. "What a mess we made of things."

He wanted to touch her so bad he shoved his hands in his pockets. Just on the shoulder or something, just to feel her warmth. "You have time for a cup of coffee?"

"Where's Willie?"

"With his friends somewhere."

He could actually see her sigh in the cold air. "We better not, Raney."

He couldn't tell whether that was a no or whether she wanted to be persuaded. But she was right; Willie could be anywhere around. He'd be willing to risk it, though, if she was. "I miss you, Carol."

"How can you miss someone you hardly had time to get used to?"

"I don't rightly know, but I do."

She turned to him, then, her eyes looking shattered. "I miss you, too."

He straightened up. It was almost more painful seeing her than not seeing her. "Maybe one of these days..." He let the words trail off.

She nodded, looking away from him again.

He could never remember feeling as desolate as he felt driving out of the station. He had lost something and hadn't gained anything in return but a son who refused to acknowledge his presence. In a way it was harder on him than when Charlene had run off. At least then he had had Willie, and it had been almost a relief to have Charlene gone.

He decided to stop by the Voyager and have a couple of drinks before heading home. Ignoring the game on TV, he drank his beer in silence and thought about Carol. What was the point in not seeing her when things seemed permanently bad with him and Willie, anyway? Willie was going to punish him the same way whether he had only seen her the once or whether he continued to see her. Might as well be hung for a sheep was his thinking by the time he had finished three beers, and he left the bar feeling more hopeful than he had felt in a long time.

CAROL HAD MEANT to shop for a Christmas present for her agent, but after seeing Raney, she drove straight home. She hadn't thought just seeing him like that would affect her, but just the sight of his face had been shattering.

She had wanted to go with him for coffee. Hell, if he'd said, "Do you want to watch me get an oil change?" she would have wanted to share it. For some reason, she hadn't realized just how much she cared until she had seen him again.

Not that it wasn't bound to happen sooner or later. It was too small a place not to run into him. She would probably run into Willie one of these days. That, however, was an encounter she wasn't looking forward to.

Not that she didn't miss him; if anything, she missed him more than Raney, only in a different way, of course. She had got so used to his afternoon visits that now she made it a habit to take a walk at the time he usually showed up. Otherwise, she found herself glued to the window in case he should pass by the cabin.

She had also been expecting Raney to stop by. She knew he probably wouldn't, that he definitely shouldn't, that she would send him away if he did. Nonetheless, something in her kept expecting it. Well, maybe not expecting; maybe just wishing.

When she got back to the cabin, she was too restless to stay inside. She went out in back of the cabin and found Mr. Rafferty's hatchet and decided she was quite capable of cutting down her own Christmas tree. There were numerous pine trees on the property, and she was sure he wouldn't mind her chopping one down.

Her adrenaline must have been flowing for some reason, because what she thought was going to be a difficult task turned out to be easy. She chopped at the poor little tree as if she had murder in mind and felled it in a matter of minutes.

She dragged it into the house and set it up in the stand she had bought, then moved it in front of the window she usually looked out of. At least she wouldn't be able to stand in front of the window anymore and watch for people who weren't going to come.

She strung the few sets of small white lights on the tree, then hung up the ornaments she had spent the last few days making. She had drawn dozens of her street kids, then colored in one item on each of them in red—a T-shirt on one, sneakers on another, red bows on a little girl's pigtails. Then she had cut them out, made holes in the top, and looped red yarn through the openings.

It only took her a few minutes to hang them all on the tree; then she plugged in the lights and stood back to view her work. She found it far more charming than her usual tree in New York with the expensive ornaments from Macy's. In fact, she thought she would talk to her agent about the idea of producing Christmas-tree ornaments from her kids next year. She thought of stuffed cotton first, then decided that wood would be more interesting. She also liked the thinness of wood; her kids were all skinny, which would be difficult to do stuffed.

Then, just when she had finally got her mind off Raney and onto something creative for a change, she heard the knock at the door and knew it was he. She knew that the chance meeting had been as traumatic for him as it had been for her.

She didn't even say anything, just opened the door and waited until he walked in. Then, wordless, they were in each other's arms. She felt unfamiliar tears threaten and fought them back with all her willpower. She was determined not to break down in front of him.

He finally released her, stepping back and looking down at her face with the kind of tenderness she had never expected from him. "I couldn't stay away," he said, a note of pleading in his voice.

"Want some coffee?" she asked, thinking it would at least prolong the time before she had to send him away again.

"I don't care. I just wanted to see you, that's all."

She went to the stove and put water on to boil; in fact, she poured enough water in the pot to take it a good ten minutes to boil. When she turned back to him, he was looking at the tree.

"That's nice," he said. "A tree makes it look like a home."

"Don't you have a tree?"

He shook his head. "Not since Charlene left. I just haven't bothered."

"You and Willie should have a tree."

"He turned to her. "Maybe; maybe we should've. But not this year. I almost wish he hadn't come home."

He looked so unhappy that she reached out and took his hands, trying to warm them in her own. "He'll come around, Raney. It's hard for a kid to keep silent for long. I know. I used to try that myself. Only sooner or later something would explode inside of me and I'd just have to talk."

"I was never like that. If I get mad, I just yell and get it all out of my system. Then I'm over it."

Carol said, "I'm more like Willie. I'm pretty good at holding a grudge."

"Remind me not to get you mad at me."

"Do you try talking to him?"

"All the time. I just carry on my end of a conversation and keep hoping he'll join in. Makes me feel foolish at times, though."

"Try the silent treatment with him. It's hard to take when you're a kid, believe me. It's easy to do yourself but not so easy when it's directed at you."

"I guess it's worth a try."

"I wish I'd never gone to that football game."

He didn't say anything, just waited.

"Not because Willie found out, although there's that. It's just that, well, before that—"

"I know. I hadn't figured us together, either."

"I didn't even like you when I met you."

Raney gave a halfhearted smile. "I wasn't much impressed by you, either. Things sure changed in a hurry, didn't they?"

She looked away from him. "Still, I guess it's better than if it had happened later. I mean, we might have fallen in love or something."

He was silent for so long she finally looked at him. He had his head cocked to one side and his lips pursed. Then his mouth releaxed, and he said, "Yeah, I guess we were lucky."

The water started to boil, and Carol fixed them each coffee. Then, as they sat down at the table together, she remembered and said, "What if Willie sees your truck out there?"

"At the moment, I don't give a damn."

"Raney, you've got to give it some time."

"My feeling on the matter right now is to say to hell with him. I want to see you."

"He loves you, Raney; it'll be okay. He's probably just as miserable as you are."

"I don't know if that's possible, Carol."

"Give it until after Christmas, anyway. What're you going to get him for Christmas?"

"I hadn't thought about it."

"It's only a couple of weeks away."

"I don't know what to get him."

"You don't have any pets, do you, Raney?" she asked, not having remembered ever seeing any around the house.

He shook his head. "Charlene never wanted any; said they were too much trouble."

"Get him a puppy. Something to love. Something he'll have responsibility for."

He smiled at that. "Don't you think that's a little obvious? In other words, show him what it's like to be a parent."

"It's obvious to you, but I don't think it'll be obvious to him. Anyway, I defy anyone to keep quiet with a puppy around."

"I don't know; we'll be going to my folks' place for Christmas."

"That's perfect, Raney. Have them pick out a puppy; that way you'll really surprise him."

"I'll think on it" was all he would say.

When he finished his coffee he said, "Now I suppose you want me to go."

She nodded. "We're adults; we can wait, Raney."

"And if it never gets better?"

"It has to."

She walked him to the door, and when they got there, he took her in his arms again and buried his face in her hair. When she moved her face to give him a kiss, she felt the wetness and looked up at him in alarm.

"What is it, Raney?"

He stood there with tears in his eyes, not even bothering to hide them. He had more guts than she did; she would've been embarrassed to let him see her cry. She pulled his mouth down to hers, then kissed him with a ferocity she didn't know was in her. Finally, he responded, holding her so tightly she could barely breathe, then once again pulling her face down against his chest and resting his head on hers.

"That's so nice," Carol said, thinking her thoughts aloud. "No man has ever cried over me before."

"I'm not made of stone, you know," he muttered.

"I guess I thought you were. I know I always try to be."

Raney pulled away from her and smiled. "Yeah, you're tough. I noticed that about you right away."

"I know you're joking, but it's the truth. I made myself that way a long time ago."

"I've seen you when you weren't so tough."

"I know, and it surprised me."

Raney sighed and reached for the door handle. "Either I go now, darlin', or I might never go."

She stepped back from him. "Don't think I wouldn't like to keep you here."

"That's nice to hear, anyway."

"Let me know if anything happens."

He nodded, then went out the door.

It was all she could do not to call him back.

RANEY TOOK Carol's suggestion and started the silent treatment that night. He didn't have much hope for it working, but he would try anything at this point. Raney was beginning to feel spooked talking to thin air all the time.

On a normal Saturday night—well, it hadn't been all that normal lately. But what he had been doing was telling Willie what time to get in, reminding him to do his homework, things like that. Willie didn't respond, but at least he knew he heard him.

But tonight he didn't do any of that. He didn't tell Willie what time to be home; he didn't tell Willie what his own plans were for the evening; he just sat across the kitchen table from him and ate his supper in silence. And then, instead of waiting it out, he left the table before Willie and left his son to do the cleaning up. At least he was still doing that, doing his share of the work around the house.

Raney had no desire to go out that night. If he couldn't see Carol, he found he had no desire to see anyone else. He would just stay home, watch TV for a while, maybe give his folks a call later and get his mom's opinion on a puppy for Willie. He wouldn't mind a puppy around; he had always had dogs around when he was a kid.

An hour later, when the front door slammed shut, he conceded that the silent treatment hadn't made a dent. He figured he would try it for a few days; then, if he still hadn't got a reponse, he'd blow off some steam and see if that worked.

And he couldn't help thinking what a waste it was that Carol was over there all alone in her cabin and he was here all alone in his house when all it would take was a few words from Willie to make them both happy.

I GUESS he got tired of talking to himself," said K.C., acting as if he were interested, but Willie could sense that his friend was getting tired of hearing about how his dad was acting toward him.

"He probably thinks the silence will get to me and I'll break down or something," said Willie.

"We could use a little silence at my house."

"I could eat another burger; how about you?" Willie asked him.

"Yeah, I could eat another."

Willie saw K.C.'s older sister, Maryann, come into the diner with her friend, Patty. Two of the most stuck up girls in school, he was thinking, remembering how Maryann had totally ignored him the whole time he was living in the same house with her. He was about to tell K.C. that his sister had just come in when he saw Maryann and Patty headed in their direction.

The two seniors paused by their booth until K.C. looked up and saw them. "What do you want, Maryann?" K.C. asked her, not acting all that interested.

"Do you know my brother K.C., Patty?" Maryann was asking the other girl.

"Yeah, I know K.C."

"And this is his friend, Willie Catlin."

Willie couldn't understand why he was being introduced to Patty, but he said, "Hi," then looked over at K.C. for guidance.

The two girls stood there for a while, but since K.C. didn't say anything, neither did Willie, and pretty soon they went away, and Willie could see them taking a booth in the back.

"What was that all about?" Willie asked K.C.

"Oh, yeah—I meant to tell you."

"Tell me what? How come Maryann's being so friendly all of a sudden?"

"Patty wanted to meet you."

Willie thought it was a joke and started to laugh.

"I mean it, Willie."

"Sure. Senior girls always go around wanting to meet sophomores. Tell me another, K.C."

"The thing is, Maryann told her about you."

"Told her what about me?"

"About you and that woman, the one your dad likes."

"So?"

"So I guess Patty figures you go for older women."

Willie wasn't quite understanding this. "What am I, a celebrity now or something?"

K.C. was grinning. "Well, you gotta realize that some of those senior girls are pretty hard up. Who've they got to date, you know? Most of the senior guys are going with younger girls."

"But Patty? She's real popular."

"That was last year."

Willie shook his head. "You telling me she's interested in me?"

K.C. shrugged. "I don't know; all I know is that she wanted to meet you. I guess she thinks she's an older woman."

"She's just as stupid as the sophomore girls."

K.C. leered. "Yeah, but she's got some body."

"I hadn't noticed." Which was a big, fat lie.

"Look at it this way, Willie. You take out a senior girl and all the sophomore girls will be falling all over you."

"I think I'm giving up girls."

"That's plain crazy. How can you give 'em up before you've even had any?'

Willie didn't have a logical answer for that.

CAROL WOULD HAVE BEEN more excited about visiting Delbert's art classes if she hadn't been afraid of running into Willie at the high school. And since the school wasn't all that large, it was a good possibility.

She had made arrangements with Delbert to lecture his eleven o'clock class, then eat lunch with the teachers. In the afternoon she would lecture two more classes.

She had prepared a short talk on her experiences in art school, then her jobs in commercial art before getting into the greeting-card business. She estimated the talk would take about twenty minutes if she took her time; then the rest of the period she would answer any questions the students might have.

She dressed in red quilted corduroy pants lined in plaid flannel and a matching vest with a heavy white turtleneck sweater underneath. With this she wore her white leather boots and her leather jacket.

Delbert must have been watching from a window, because as soon as she pulled into the parking lot, she saw him come out of a door and head in her direction. She thought he must be freezing without a coat on, so she got out of the car fast and hurried over to him.

"I was afraid you wouldn't come," he told her.

"I told you I would."

"Yeah, but I thought you might've chickened out."

"I'm looking forward to it. I like kids."

"Don't say that around the other teachers; they'll think you have a screw loose."

He shepherded her into the building and down to the teachers' room, where he hung up her coat. Then, looking her over, he said, "You look great. You can sure tell you buy your clothes in New York."

Carol was surprised. It was the first time anyone in Rock Ridge had said anything about her clothes, and most of the time she felt she was getting strange looks. "Thanks."

"I wish I could afford a leather jacket like that."

Carol smiled. "I think the more they distress the leather, the more they charge for them. It costs money to look poor."

Delbert laughed. "It's funny, when you're really poor, you don't want clothes that look old. I know that's the fashion, though."

He took her down to his classroom, and she looked around at some of the students' work while they waited for the next class to arrive. He kept trying to put her at her ease, which was beginning to make her nervous.

When the class finally filed in and Delbert had taken attendance and introduced her, Carol stood up and smiled at the class. Since it was art, they were seated at tables rather than desks, and she pulled over a stool and sat down on it.

She gave her prepared speech, and all the kids listened attentively, but they didn't seem very interested. They were quiet and polite, but most of the faces looked blank.

She ended it with, "Do you have any questions?" Then she waited for the response.

None came.

Not knowing what to do, she turned to Delbert. "Hey," he said to the kids, "you guys usually never shut up. Isn't there anything you'd like to ask her?"

The class loosened up a little then, and there was some laughter, but still no hands went up in the air. Then, just when she was wondering what she could talk about for the rest of the period, one boy in the back raised his hand.

"Yes?" said Carol.

"When you were in art school, did you ever have nude models?"

There was a shocked silence for a moment, then a burst of giggles from some of the girls. Most of the boys were outwardly smirking.

Carol suppressed her own smile and said, "Yes, we frequently had nude models. Both male and female. That's standard in art school."

"Weren't you embarrassed?" asked one of the girls, who then covered her mouth with her hand.

Carol did smile then. "Yes, at first. I think everyone in the class was. But after a while it just seemed natural."

Then another hand shot up, and Carol thought the face looked familiar. "Could you draw some pictures of us?" the boy asked, and Carol belatedly recognized him as one of the children at Donna Lee's for Thanksgiving.

Carol looked over at Delbert, and he spread his arms and shrugged.

"I tell you what," Carol said. "I'll draw you if you'll draw me."

And so for the remainder of the period she did quick sketches of the class while they sat at the tables and drew her drawing them.

"These are priceless," she told Delbert after the class had left. They were looking over the sketches the kids had handed in.

"You're lucky a couple of them didn't draw you nude," he said, making her laugh.

"What do you suggest I do for the other two classes? Obviously the question period isn't going to take the time I allotted it."

"You could have them try their hand at greeting cards."

"Good idea."

She enjoyed eating lunch with the teachers. She wasn't sure if they were actually as interesting as she thought they were or whether she was just starved for company, but she found herself doing more talking than she had in ages. She also saw how well liked Delbert was and found she liked him quite a bit herself. She was really hoping they could be friends.

The afternoon classes went better. With them she also brought out some of her greeting cards to pass around. She hadn't done it in the first class because it felt to her like showing off, but she found it started a discussion about the differences between kids in New York and kids in Georgia that everyone found entertaining.

When the greeting cards the kids had done were turned in, Carol was amazed at how clever some of them were. "I might steal some of these ideas," she told Delbert.

"I wouldn't if I were you; they were probably stolen in the first place."

Carol was feeling lucky when Delbert walked her out to her car after school. The classes had gone all right, and she hadn't run into Willie. But sure enough, just as she was feeling that, she noticed the group of kids surrounding her car, and Willie was one of them.

"You can't blame them," said Delbert. "It's not often they see a Mercedes."

Carol could see Willie watching her approach and didn't know how to handle it. She finally decided to just be polite and ask him how he was, but when she got close enough to him to say anything, he turned on his heels and walked off. For a moment she considered going after him but decided that would probably just embarrass him.

Delbert beat her to the car door and opened it for her. "Is it still on for Saturday night?" he asked her.

She remembered the school play. "Sure. You want me to meet you here?"

He looked as if he were about to argue, then changed his mind. "Fine. Maybe we could get a bite to eat afterward."

"Sounds good," she told him.

"Then how about seven forty-five at the front entrance?"

Carol agreed; then Delbert shooed the kids away from the car so she could drive off.

As she drove home, she found she was envying Delbert. The trouble with working free-lance at home was the lack of interaction with other people in the same line of work. Once that had seemed a plus; now she wasn't so sure the reclusive life suited her.

Maybe she would look into teaching an art course somewhere or even giving private lessons. She had a feeling, though, that Rock Ridge wasn't the right place for it.

Chapter Eleven

It had been snowing all day, and by midafternoon of the shortest day of the year the view from her cabin looked like a Christmas card. Even her car was almost blotted out of the landscape by the snow covering it. It did seem criminal to leave such an expensive car outdoors to rust, and she thought of buying some kind of tarpaulin with which to cover it. But not today. It still hadn't stopped snowing, and she didn't want to shovel a path to the car twice.

She thought about going out and enjoying the snow for a little while but decided against it. It was almost dark out, and she could tell the temperature was dropping rapidly; plus a wicked wind could be heard outside whistling around the corners of the cabin.

She put a TV dinner in the toaster oven and a pot of water to boil on the hot plate. It was almost Christmas, and she was as ready for it as she ever was.

Her Christmas cards had been mailed, as had the present she had sent to her agent. She had told Donna Lee she would love to spend Christmas with her and her family. It wasn't so much that she would love to as she was grateful that she wouldn't have to spend it alone. She had insisted on bringing something for the dinner, and Donna Lee had told her she could provide the dessert if she wished. Carol had placed an order at the local bakery for five different pies: two pumpkin, one mince and two chocolate, because she could remember hating pumpkin and mince as a child.

She wasn't looking forward to Christmas Eve. She supposed she would end up watching all the Christmas shows on television that people all alone on the holidays watched. She would have considered braving the Voyager that night, knowing Raney would be out of town, only she had a feeling that a small-town bar wouldn't stay open Christmas Eve.

She might have invited Delbert over that evening except that he was going to Atlanta to spend the holidays with his sister. She chided herself for caring; the past few Christmases in New York she had spent alone and hadn't minded. She thought it might have something to do with the fact that in New York so many people spent the holidays alone. Here it was practically all families, and even the few people who lived alone had relatives nearby to go to.

She wondered what Mr. Rafferty had done for Christmas. J. J. Rafferty, however, appeared to have more success with being a recluse than she did. Maybe it would just take a few more years of practice.

The cabin was getting chilly even with both heaters on high, so after she ate, she opened the couch and got out the electric blanket she had bought and not yet used. She put her Christmas cassette on, piled a bunch of unread magazines on the bed and got under the blanket to read.

When she felt herself falling to sleep over the printed word, she reached out and turned off the lamp next to the couch, too lazy to get up and douse the Christmas-tree lights. Anyway, she liked the looks of the fairy-tale lights on the tree.

She didn't know how long she had slept, but she woke up freezing cold and in the dark. She knew she should have known better than to have everything electric going at once.

She got up and felt her way to the circuit-breaker box next to the kitchen sink. She opened it and pulled each lever, but nothing happened. She felt lucky it wasn't the old-fashioned type with fuses; it was the same kind she had in her New York apartment, and she couldn't figure out why it didn't work.

She considered herself a practical person, one with foresight, but in this case she had fallen down. She had neither flashlight nor candles in the cabin.

She came to the conclusion that she had two options. She could stand around freezing to death while she flipped the switches all night, or she could bundle up and get back into bed and try to find an electrician in the morning.

She put on three pairs of socks, sweat pants and two sweatshirts over her pajamas and got back into bed. And then she remembered what Raney had said about blackouts.

She had no way of knowing whether it was a blackout or whether she was the only one without electricity. She didn't have a phone to call and find out, and she had no batteries for her radio. She couldn't see any houses from her windows, and even if she could, it was four o'clock in the morning, something she had found out when she held her lighter to her watch.

She wondered how long it would take to freeze to death, which was being overly pessimistic, because there were plenty of things she could burn in the fireplace if she really got desperate. Like an entire wall of books. Only she would hate to burn anything of Mr. Rafferty's unless it were actually a matter of life and death. Which it wasn't. Not yet, anyway.

She couldn't get back to sleep; in fact, she was afraid to go back to sleep. People did freeze to death in their sleep, didn't they? It was the longest night she could ever remember spending.

Eventually, though, she could see the room gradually becoming lighter, and she got out of bed and went to the window. It was so frosted over she couldn't see out, and her immediate thought of using her hair dryer to defrost the window died when she realized it ran on electricity.

She tried the circuit breakers a few more times, then put on her boots and her parka and decided she would at least be warmer in her car. It was filled with gas and had an excellent heater.

She unlocked the door and went to push it open, and absolutely nothing happened. She couldn't remember whether wood expanded or contracted in the cold, but hers had obviously expanded, because it wouldn't budge. Which was just great, just what she needed. That's when she began to get mad.

She pushed aside the kitchen table and opened the window. And all she saw was a wall of snow. Which was ridiculous; it couldn't have snowed several feet in one night, could it?

She closed the window, stood on a kitchen chair and pulled down the top part of the window. This part was at least clear of snow, but she looked out at an almost unbelievable scene. Drifts of snow were piled up against the cabin, and she couldn't even see her car, not even the shape of it. Except for the bare tops of trees, everything was white as far as she could see.

She stepped up onto the windowsill and started to crawl out the window. Only she didn't balance as she had planned and fell head first into the snow. She got up, brushing the snow out of her eyes, and felt better. At least she didn't feel like a prisoner anymore.

There was a new problem. If she was successful at finding her car and clearing it of snow, she had left the car keys in the cabin, along with her cigarettes. Still, she reasoned that if she had got out once, she could get out again, and she tried to get back in the window. It was a useless struggle, though. The more she tried, the farther she sank down in the snow, until she couldn't even reach the top of the window anymore.

She looked in the direction of the road but couldn't see it. Which meant the snowplows hadn't been out yet. Eventually, she was sure they would go by her cabin, and then maybe she could get a ride with them into town. She didn't know how that would be an improvement except that she at least could sit in the diner and be warm while she figured out what to do. Unless the town was also blacked out.

Still, she wasn't a helpless female. She hated helpless females. If she was in an untenable situation, then she would just get herself out of it. And the first thing to do would be to find the snow shovel and clear the door to the cabin. At least she had left that unlocked. And then the second thing she would do would be to cut herself some wood for the fireplace.

And after that was all done, she would go back to bed and get some sleep.

RANEY WAS GOING to bed so early these days he was waking up early. He knew something was wrong when he looked at his alarm clock and it said 4:10 and yet it was light out. Power failure, he instantly surmised, and got out of bed and tried the lights. It happened too frequently for him to assume it was only his lights out.

Which was one advantage of a wood furnace. It didn't depend on electricity. Nor did his gas stove, and he went downstairs and put some water on to boil. That was when he looked out the kitchen window and saw the extent of the snowstorm. The TV had predicted several inches last night, but it had been so windy the drifts were more like several feet.

And then he thought of Carol. He remembered warning her about blackouts, about promising to cut her firewood and then never doing it. At this moment she could be trapped in her cabin, freezing to death. And he knew he was partially responsible.

He turned off the stove and rushed upstairs. Not even thinking about the fact that neither of them was speaking to the other, he went into Willie's room and shook him awake.

Willie opened his eyes and turned an angry look on him.

"The power's off, and Carol's probably snowed in and without any heat. And all because neither of us cut her any logs after she bought those electric heaters. Come on; I'm going to need your help."

Raney dressed in his warmest clothes, including long underwear, and by the time he was dressed, Willie was downstairs putting on his jacket.

Their front door opened inward, so they were able to open it, but it took a good ten minutes to clear away enough snow to get out. The walk to her cabin, which should have taken another five minutes, took more like twenty-five, as they had to contend with snowdrifts and unplowed roads all the way.

When they finally reached her cabin, Raney saw the open window, the cleared doorway and the footsteps reaching around the cabin, and he felt himself shaking with relief. With Willie behind him, he followed her footsteps until he found her shoveling snow away from a large tree, a hatchet lying by her side.

They were silent in the snow, but she must have heard his heavy breathing, because she turned around, her eyes widening. "Is it a blackout?" was the first thing she asked.

He nodded, too winded to speak.

"Hi, Willie," she said, looking past him.

Willie seemed to say, "Hi," automatically, then remember that he wasn't speaking these days and shut up.

"You better come on home with us," said Raney.

He saw that stubborn, determined tomboyish look of hers come over her face, with the lower lip pushing out. He felt like laughing out loud and kissing her at the same time.

"Did you come over to save me?" she asked.

"I thought you might need some help. I figured you never got around to getting yourself some firewood."

"No. I got an electric blanket instead," she said with a rueful look.

"Come on; our house is warm. We've got a wood-burning furnace and a gas stove at least."

"I'm managing fine," she told him. "I've cleared the door, and as soon as I cut some firewood, I'm going to clear my car of snow and go to town."

"You're coming home with us," said Raney. "It'd take you all day to cut down that tree there, and even then it'll probably be too wet to burn."

Carol looked from him to Willie and back again. "I'll get it burning with some magazines."

Raney reached out and grabbed the shovel from her hands and threw it down on the ground. "Will you quit being so god-awful stubborn and just listen to me for a minute? I'd have done the same for J.J., I'd do the same for any neighbor. No one's asking you to give up your independence and integrity; all I'm doing is offering you a warm place to stay until they get the electricity on again. For all I care, you can lock yourself up in one of the rooms and sulk. But you're coming with us, you hear?" And without waiting for any argument, he grabbed her by the wrist and began to pull her away from the tree.

She made her body dead weight, and he saw the imploring look she threw at Willie. And then the kid said an entire sentence.

"Come on," said Willie. "At least you'll get some breakfast."

Carol's look of stubborn determination wavered. "All right, but let go of my wrist."

Raney let go and let her fall to the ground. Getting up, she gave him a sheepish grin and admitted, "I could sure use some coffee."

Raney felt so unaccountably pleased that she was coming home with him that he found himself hoping the electricity would stay off a good while. Then again, she wouldn't even know when it came on unless someone told her.

CAROL HAD LONG BEEN CURIOUS to see Raney's house. To see it in the company of two people estranged because of her, though, wasn't an ideal circumstance.

The first thing she noticed about the house was the warmth. The second was the darkness of the entry hall. The third was the totally cluttered hallway he led her down to get to the kitchen.

The kitchen was great. The big window let in light, and the room was huge, with a round table and six chairs and even a rocking chair in one corner. It looked clean, too, but like the hall, it was terribly cluttered. All kinds of things that belonged in a kitchen and all kinds of things that didn't belong in a kitchen were blended together in what could have passed as a secondhand store.

Raney put on coffee, telling her to get out of her boots and jacket. She did, but her socks and her pants were soaked right through. And under her pants were her flannel pajamas.

Willie was hanging around the kitchen door, and when Raney said, "Willie, find her some dry clothes to wear," he disappeared, and Carol could hear footsteps going up the stairs.

"Things are no better?" she asked him softly.

He shook his head. "I took your advice and gave him the silent treatment, but except that it's easier, it hasn't changed anything."

"Maybe Christmas will help."

"I'm getting him a puppy like you suggested."

"That ought to work, if anything," she said, then stopped whispering as Raney came over to her and took her in his arms. For a long, lovely, warm moment she luxuriated in the feel of his body next to hers and his breath in her hair; then they both pulled back.

"God, how I've thought about you," murmured Raney, looking so profoundly sad she wanted to hug him again. But Willie could be back any second, and she didn't want to make things worse.

She just said, "So have I," wondering if she looked as sad as he did.

Carol was drinking coffee in gulps when Willie came back down carrying jeans and a high-school sweatshirt. Raney pointed out the downstairs bathroom to her, and she went inside to change.

The pants were a good fit with the legs rolled up, and the sweatshirt was fine. She looked in the mirror, saw her red face and thought it looked pretty healthy, then wondered if she could have frostbite. She was pretty sure you felt numb with frostbite, though, and her face felt all prickly.

When she got back to the kitchen, Willie was at the table eating cold cereal, and Raney was cooking bacon and eggs. Without asking, she found the bread and started to make toast. No one was talking, so she just went ahead and buttered it and took some plates out, then sat down at the table and waited for her breakfast.

"Hope you don't mind them scrambled," said Raney, scooping some onto a plate along with bacon and handing it to her.

"At this point I'd eat anything," she told him. "But no, I don't mind them scrambled. Anything but poached."

"I don't know how to poach 'em," said Raney.

She ate everything on her plate before asking, "How long does it usually stay off?"

"Anywhere from a few minutes to a few hours."

"We could always play cards," she said, picturing a cozy scene of being snowed in. After all, being snowed in with Raney was a recurring fantasy of hers. Being snowed in with Raney and Willie, however, wasn't. Hence, the cards.

"Too much work to do. We're going to have to clear the driveway and the truck. Then, if the snowplows get through, we'll take some logs over to your place. Hell, I forgot all about closing that window of yours."

"It doesn't matter. It's not snowing anymore, and it couldn't get any colder inside. You want some help shoveling?"

He shook his head. "Only got two shovels. You just stay in here and keep warm. If you need to feel useful, you can do the dishes."

She thought she would prefer shoveling to doing dishes, but on the other hand, she still wasn't completely warmed up. While Raney and Willie got back into their jackets and boots, she cleared off the table, then watched them go back out of the house.

She did the dishes and stacked them to dry in the drainer, then went back down the hall and into the living room. Looking out the front window, she could see Raney and Willie at work trying to unbury the truck. Knowing she wouldn't be disturbed for a while, she decided to take a look at the house.

She found the living room claustrophobic. It shouldn't have been, because it was a large room, but like the kitchen and hall, it was cluttered. Perhaps it would look better with some lamps lit; the dark paneling on the walls gave it a closed-in feeling that she didn't experience in her much smaller cabin.

There was too much furniture for one thing, and none of it seemed to match, as though the contents from several houses had been brought together to furnish the room. On the floor beside one chair newspapers were stacked at least two feet high. Dozens of needlepoint cushions were strewn around on chairs and sofas.

She would have straightened it up if it had needed straightening, but it didn't. The place was neat and appeared clean; it just had too much stuff around. On top of the large TV set and all over the wall above it were photographs in dime-store frames. She looked at

them, but there wasn't enough light to see them
clearly. One was a wedding portrait, though, and she
had no trouble recognizing a younger Raney, particularly since Willie was the image of his father. All she
could tell about Charlene as a bride was that she was
well-endowed and blond.

There was a dining room across the hall from the
living room that didn't look used. It held heavy ma-
hogany furniture that could be antique, and the table
could easily seat twelve.

She remembered Donna Lee saying that Raney
made furniture. If so, it wasn't in any of the rooms she
had seen. She thought of going upstairs but decided
that would definitely be snooping.

She went back to the kitchen and had another cup
of coffee and a cigarette. She felt warm now and rested
and was beginning to be bored. Being snowed in at
Raney's house was no better than being snowed in at
her own if she was going to be left alone. Furthermore, it didn't seem right that they should have to do
all the work while she sat around doing nothing.

She turned on the oven and left the door open,
hanging her wet socks on a chair where the heat could
get to them. In just a few minutes they seemed to be
dry, and she put them on along with her boots and
parka, then went out the front door to see if she could
be of any help.

They had uncovered the truck and were shoveling a
path down to the road. Still, the snowplow hadn't
come by, and they would be unable to drive it until
that occurred.

"Do you have a sled?" Carol asked Raney.

He turned around and frowned. "Go back in the house before you catch cold," he told her, sounding rather like a parent.

"I'm perfectly dry, and there's nothing to do in there. Do you have a sled?"

"What do you want with a sled?"

"I thought, if you could spare them, that I could carry a load of logs over to the cabin and try to get it heated up."

Raney's look of annoyance turned to one of admiration. He had obviously thought she had sledding down a hill in mind. "There's one in the shed behind the house. Go help her tie down some logs, Willie."

"If you'll just tell me where some rope is, I can do it myself," said Carol.

Raney stared at her; she stared right back, and he finally grinned. "Okay, be independent. You'll find some rope in one of the kitchen drawers. If you do need some help, though, just holler."

"I sure will, Raney," she said, letting him know by her tone that she was quite capable of such a simple task.

"Sometimes people are just too independent for their own good," she could hear him clearly say as she turned and walked back to the house. Willie didn't say anything.

THE THING WAS, it had been exactly the kind of situation Willie had been fantasizing about for weeks—a situation in which Carol was in danger and needed help and he, naturally, would be the one to rescue her.

Only it hadn't worked out that way.

For one thing, his dad had sensed the danger first and had asked for his help instead of Willie sensing it and doing it alone. And then, when they got over there to rescue her, she hadn't even needed rescuing. In fact, Willie figured she would have made out just fine without them.

And the thing about taking logs over to her cabin on a sled—that made a lot of sense. He wished he had been the one to think of it. Sure, they could carry more logs in the truck, but then again, the truck wasn't going anywhere.

They were still shoveling a path to the road twenty minutes later when Carol came around the side of the house with a load of logs on his sled. She left the sled there and disappeared, appearing again a few minutes later with his toboggan, also with a load of logs on it. Pulling the toboggan up to them, she let go of the rope and said, "Do you have a thermos I could borrow? I thought I could take some hot water over for some coffee."

His dad just said, "Cupboard over the refrigerator," and Carol headed back to the house.

Without looking at him, his dad said, "She's going to insist on pulling those herself if we wait for her." Then Raney took hold of the rope and started off with the toboggan.

Willie went back and took hold of the rope tied to the sled and followed the path his dad was making. It only made sense that they be the ones to pull them. He knew that Carol would have insisted on doing it herself, but if they were halfway there by the time she came out, there wasn't anything she could do about it.

He couldn't help seeing the way his dad looked at Carol and the way she looked back at him. To be fair, he knew they weren't doing it on purpose to make him mad or anything. He guessed they couldn't help themselves.

It surprised him the way his dad was looking at her. He looked as if he really cared, kind of like the way he remembered his dad looking at his mom before she got strange. And Carol was looking at his dad the way Willie wished just once she would look at him. Well, that was their problem. They would get over it just the way he was getting over it.

And that part really surprised him. He found that in his daydreams of Carol he liked her a whole lot more than he was actually liking her now in person. In his mind he had made her into some perfect kind of person when in actuality she was just human like everyone else.

Still, he had to admit she was braver and more resourceful than most women would have been. They would have just sat around crying and waiting to be saved, while Carol had been out there saving herself. Still, that didn't leave much for a guy to do.

Willie was worried that maybe the snowplows wouldn't come through. It was Christmas vacation, and there was a party tonight he really wanted to go to. One of the seniors on the football team was having it, and it would be one of the few parties in which different classes mixed. He knew from K.C. that Patty was going to be there; in fact, K.C. must've mentioned it at least a hundred times.

He hadn't taken it seriously the night K.C. had told him Patty had wanted to meet him. He figured it was just K.C.'s way of getting his mind off Carol.

He had started to believe him, though, when at school Patty said hi to him every time they passed each other in the halls. The first time he was too surprised to say anything; after that, though, he would say hi back and watch the looks he got from the kids in his class. It wasn't often a senior girl said hi to a sophomore boy.

He couldn't help noticing how good-looking Patty was. She had a lot of long, blond, naturally curly hair, a cute, turned-up nose and the kind of smile that showed off her white teeth. Of course, some guys wouldn't even notice her face, because she had the kind of shape that had K.C. goggling most of the time. Plus she wore really tight sweaters and skirts that fit so snugly she had trouble walking in them.

He personally thought Carol had a lot more class. Still, as K.C. said, class wasn't everything.

He figured that if she was really interested in him, he'd give her a chance. He wouldn't fall in love with her or anything, but he wouldn't mind taking her out a few times. Being a senior and one who had gone steady her junior year, she must have had a lot of experience. And experience was something Willie desired. And maybe when he got some experience, he would at least know how to act with Carol if he was ever alone with her again.

He had this recent daydream in which Carol found out that he was seeing Patty and got jealous and realized what she had lost and begged him to forgive her.

That particular daydream was pretty satisfying even though he knew it would never happen. Even though he wished that it were different, he knew that Carol had only thought of him as a friend. Carol had never—even once—looked at him the way she looked at his father.

Still, if he couldn't have her, he sure wasn't going to let his dad. If he couldn't have her, then he wished she would just go back to New York so everyone could forget all about her.

Chapter Twelve

The electricity came back on at one o'clock, went off again briefly about twenty minutes later, but by two it was restored. At three-thirty the snowplow cleared the road to town.

While Raney and Willie were busy cutting her a supply of logs, Carol cleared her car of snow and shoveled a path out to the road. When the road was cleared, she drove to the general store in order to buy candles and a flashlight. If it turned out to be anything like New York, there would never be a blackout as long as she was prepared for it, but that was all right with her.

There was a festive atmosphere in the store, and she couldn't tell whether it was due to the holiday season or whether, like New York, people were drawn closer in times of emergency.

People she didn't even know asked her how she had fared all alone in her cabin and then laughed with glee when she told them about her useless electric heaters and blanket. They clearly found humor in city peoples' ideas of roughing it in the country.

She wouldn't have presumed to buy Christmas presents for Raney or Willie, although before the difficulties she certainly would have got something for each of them. Now, however, she felt she owed them something for all their help. They had spent hours of their time helping her out, and she wanted to thank them with some kind of gift.

She found Holly's General Store amazing. It carried everything from cat food to skis, from cosmetics to boots, and she walked around now looking for something she could get them. Raney was easy. She didn't want to make the gift personal and have it misconstrued by Willie, so she got him a case of Jack Daniel's. She didn't think one bottle was enough and liked the idea of an entire case.

Willie was more difficult. She would have liked to get him a warm cable-knit sweater she saw, but thought it was too much like the kind of gift a parent would buy a child. She finally decided on a Sony Walkman, something she knew he didn't have and that she thought any teenage boy might like.

She got a few strange looks when she asked for the case of Jack Daniel's, but she didn't explain that it wasn't for her even though she knew she was leaving the owners with the impression she was a rather heavy drinker.

When she got home, she rebuilt the fire in the fireplace even though the heaters were on and also lit a few of the candles she had bought. They looked festive, and she felt well prepared in case of another blackout.

She sat down at her drawing table and drew two cards. The one for Raney had a comical drawing of her plunging head first out the window of the cabin into the snow. The one for Willie had a picture of him felling a tree that was just about to fall on top of her cabin. Inside both of them she wrote "Thanks" and then signed her name.

She then drove down to their house, saw that the truck wasn't there and quickly carried the gifts up to the front door where they'd be seen. She only hoped that they wouldn't have the kind of pride where they would insist on returning them to her.

THE PARTY WAS JUMPING by the time Willie and K.C. got there. Everyone was talking about the snowstorm, and each had a blackout story to tell.

Willie checked out the whereabouts of Patty right away, and when he saw she was with some of the other senior girls, talking, he went over and joined some of the basketball players. Except for a couple of guys, the basketball team was made up of the same players as the football team had been.

Willie was wearing his Sony Walkman. He thought it looked cool to wear it even though he didn't have it playing at the moment. The guys noticed it right away, and they all wanted to try it on for a minute, and Willie let them pass it around.

When he and his dad found the presents in front of the house and took them inside and opened them, Willie was afraid his dad was going to say they had to give them back. But all Raney had done was broken open one of the bottles of Jack Daniel's and had a drink straight from the bottle, so Willie felt free to try out the Walkman.

He thought it was a neat present, maybe the neatest he had ever got. It really showed she cared for him, too, to have got him something like that, something that cost a lot of bucks.

Of course he would have really been a sensation if he had walked into the party carrying a case of Jack Daniel's. That really would've got passed around. Still, he could see there was a lot of beer around, and he really didn't like the taste of whiskey, anyway.

Tommy was giving the party, and he told everyone that his folks had gone to the city to do some last-minute Christmas shopping and he figured they wouldn't get back before eleven at the earliest. Which gave everyone plenty of time to get good and high before Tommy's folks put a stop to the drinking.

The guys were mostly just standing around with beer cans in their hands, shooting the bull, while the girls were putting records on the stereo and dancing with each other. He knew, though, that as soon as the guys had consumed enough beer, they'd be asking the girls to dance. Not that they were all that hot on dancing, but it was the easiest way to get close to a girl without having to actually date her.

Willie caught Patty looking at him twice, and he wasn't just imagining it, either, because the second time she smiled at him and wet her lips with her tongue. He played it cool and didn't even smile back at her, but he made sure she knew he had seen her.

About twenty minutes after Willie and K.C. had got there, the doorbell rang, and in walked Marla and

Suzanna, the two girls with the worst reputations in school. He could see right away that the other girls were really put out; they got together in a huddle, and Willie was afraid for a while that they were going to decide to leave. They didn't, though, although they sure put up a show of ignoring Marla and Suzanna.

Willie couldn't help noticing what the two newcomers were wearing as soon as they got out of their coats and boots. Unlike the other girls, who were mostly in jeans or sweaters and wool skirts, Marla and Suzanna looked as if they were going to a disco or something. They had on really high heels and stockings with designs on them, skirts practically up to their rear ends and low-cut sweaters that showed for sure that they weren't wearing bras.

Willie looked over at K.C., ready to make a remark, and saw that K.C. was all but drooling. "Your mouth's hanging open," Willie told him.

K.C. poked him in the ribs and grinned. "I'd like to get me some of that tonight."

"I'm sure they're here for the seniors."

"I don't mind waiting my turn, Willie."

Things changed pretty fast then as most of the boys started dancing with the girls. Willie saw that Patty wasn't dancing and decided to make his move.

He walked over to her and said, "Wanna dance?" and she moved out to the center of the room with him without saying anything.

Willie didn't consider himself much of a dancer, but he could move around to the music okay. Patty, though, was really good. He had noticed that girls usually danced one of two ways. Either they moved their hips a lot, or they moved the tops of their bodies. Patty moved the top of her body, and since she had a whole lot on top, it was pretty distracting to watch.

He figured she was wearing a bra, because she was built really big and she was one of the nice girls, but the bra couldn't have done too much for her, because her boobs were really bouncing around. He had a lot of trouble keeping his eyes off them, but when he finally looked up and saw that Patty was watching him, all she did was smile, as if she wanted him to look at her, as if she got a charge out of it.

Some smart guy, who Willie guessed couldn't wait any longer, stopped the record in the middle and put on a slow song. Almost simultaneously, most of the lights in the room were turned off. Before Willie had even decided what to do, Patty moved in close to him and wrapped her arms around his neck.

He put his arms around her waist and rested his head on hers, extremely conscious of the fact that her boobs were pressed up tight against his chest. He looked around and saw that most of the guys had their hands on their partners' rear ends, so Willie moved his hands down. He half expected Patty to tell him to cut it out; instead, she moved in even closer to him.

It was beginning to get really warm in the room. What was worse, Willie was beginning to get really turned on. And he didn't see how Patty could help but notice, since she was plastered against him.

She didn't even move back, though, just pressed against him harder, and Willie began to feel things he had previously only imagined feeling.

Most of the kids weren't even making a pretense of dancing anymore. Mostly they were just locked in each other's arms, and he could see a lot of them were kissing. Willie moved his head off the top of Patty's head, and right away she looked up at him with her eyes closed and her mouth parted.

He started kissing her, and her tongue immediately came out, and so he opened his mouth and waited to see what she would do. What she did was stick her tongue right in his mouth and start moving it around, and Willie could feel himself breaking out in a sweat.

Then Patty removed one of her arms from around his neck and reached behind her and grabbed one of his hands. In a maneuver that nearly demolished him, she pulled his hand around between them and stuck it up inside her sweater. The next thing he knew, his hand was over the front of her bra.

At that point Willie was pretty sure he was in love.

CAROL WAS CURLED UP on the couch watching "How the Grinch Stole Christmas" when Raney knocked.

She opened the door, and he was standing there with a bottle of Jack Daniel's in his hand and a big grin on his face. She looked past him and said, "Where's your truck?"

"I was too drunk to drive," he said, slurring his words.

"I can see I bought you the wrong thing."

"Not at all," he said, squeezing past her into the room. "You bought me exactly the right thing. Furthermore, I took it as an invitation."

Carol said, "It wasn't meant to be."

"Certainly it was. You didn't want me to drink alone, did you?"

"Can I get you a glass and some ice?"

"No, thanks. It got cold sitting outside." He handed her the bottle, but she shook her head.

His face fell. "You're not going to drink with me?"

"How about if I have some wine?"

"Will it get you drunk?"

"If I drink enough of it."

"Okay. Get yourself some wine." She saw him move over to see what she was watching, then said, "The Grinch! You're watching the Grinch!"

"What's Christmas without the Grinch?" said Carol, pouring herself a glass of wine.

"I love the Grinch."

He sounded so much like a little kid that she laughed. "Good. Sit down and you can watch it with me."

"I haven't seen the Grinch in years," he said, almost falling onto the couch, then righting himself.

"It's on every year."

"Is it? Every year?"

She nodded, sitting down beside him.

"I can't think of anyone I'd rather watch the Grinch with," he said, looking at her with great sincerity.

"Would you like me to fix you some coffee, Raney?"

"Coffee? You think I'm drunk?"

Carol kept silent.

"You're right; I am drunk. I got drunk because you bought me such a nice gift."

Carol patted his arm. "Keep quiet and watch the Grinch."

"I don't want to keep quiet. I got drunk on purpose so I could talk to you."

"I thought you liked the Grinch."

He got to his feet and unsteadily made his way to the TV set. With a flourish, he turned it off, then turned to face her, a happy smile on his face.

"Raney, please let me make you some coffee."

"You're sounding like a wife, Carol."

She felt herself stiffen, then saw the gleam in his eyes and relaxed. She finished her wine and said, "Have another drink, Raney," and got up to get herself more wine. He was obviously determined to get as drunk as possible. As long as he didn't pass out in her place, she thought he might as well have his wish. She wouldn't mind getting a little drunk herself.

He wandered over to where she was pouring the wine and watched her. "I had to drink so I could get up my nerve to talk to you."

"I never noticed you were shy, Raney."

He chuckled. "I'm not shy. What makes you think I'm shy?"

"I don't think you're shy. But why did you need to drink to talk to me?"

"I can't remember. I know that was my plan, but I can't remember why. Do you know why?"

She took his hand and led him back to the couch. "Did it have anything to do with Willie?"

"What about Willie?"

"That's what I'm asking you, Raney. Did you want to talk to me about Willie?"

"Hell, no! Can't we for once not talk about Willie?"

She sighed. "Is he out tonight?"

"Of course he's out. If he weren't, I wouldn't be here, would I?"

She put down her glass of wine and put her arms around him, resting her cheek against his. "Oh, Raney, what're we going to do?"

"About what?"

She gave him an exasperated look. "About us. About your having to sneak out to see me."

"I didn't sneak out. I walked right out the door."

It wasn't any good talking to him; he was too drunk. She wished he had come over sober, although even sober there wouldn't be a solution. She might as well just hold him and enjoy the moment while it lasted. She leaned up, gave him a kiss on the lips, then rested her head on his chest.

"You know what I'd really love to do, darlin'?" he said, his voice sounding wistful.

She was pretty sure it was the same thing she'd like to do. She snuggled closer to him and said, "What would you like to do, Raney?"

He moved away from her a little and looked into her eyes. "I'd love to build a snowman."

She just stared at him. That was maybe the last thing she had expected him to come up with. "Are you serious, Raney?"

"Dead serious. Come on. Bundle up, put on your mittens, and we'll go outside and build the biggest damn snowman in Georgia. Hell, in the world!"

IT WAS ABOUT TEN O'CLOCK when Patty pulled Willie into the hall closet and shut the door. They had been dancing steadily, if you could call it dancing. Willie didn't call it dancing; he called it making out standing up.

Now Patty had him in a closet that was pitch dark, and she was pulling him down on the floor so that he was lying on what felt like someone's rubber boots. He was about to complain when Patty moved down on top of him and he no longer felt like complaining.

"I find you very exciting," she whispered in his ear. Then she lifted herself up a little, and when she lowered herself, his hands, which had been on his chest, were now against bare flesh. He felt a shudder go through him.

He didn't know whether he was supposed to say anything. He was glad she found him exciting; he had always thought he was pretty boring.

"I heard all about it," she was saying. "How you broke up some romance between your father and some woman, how she preferred you. What kind of things did you do with her?"

Willie thought it would be prudent not to straighten her out on her facts. "Oh, different things," he said, trying to sound normal.

"Like this?" she asked, moving one of his hands up her skirt while he lay wide-eyed in anticipation.

"Yeah, well, sometimes," he managed to say. As though he did it all the time, his other hand was now squeezing one of her boobs. He couldn't believe how big it was. She must have the biggest pair in the school.

"How're you getting home?" she asked him.

"Uh, we were hoping to get a ride."

"Want me to drive you home?"

"Yeah, sure."

Patty moved away from him, and he could tell she was straightening her clothes. "Let's get out of here, okay?"

"Yeah, I'm ready to go."

A couple of the girls were walking by when Patty opened the closet door, and Willie felt kind of stupid being caught in a closet like that, particularly with Patty still adjusting her bra. Oh, jeez, she wasn't adjusting it; she was taking it off. Now she was pulling it out from under her sweater and stuffing it in her shoulder bag.

She looked different without a bra. She looked even bigger, for one thing, and about four inches lower. He couldn't believe he had actually squeezed them.

"Let me go tell K.C. I'm leaving," he said to her; then, worried she might change her mind, he asked, "You'll wait here, won't you?"

"I'll be right here," she said in a whispery kind of voice guaranteed to keep him excited.

"Where'd you disappear to?" K.C. asked him when Willie had located him in the kitchen.

"You wouldn't believe me if I told you."

K.C. smiled wickedly. "Try me."

"I was in the closet with Patty."

"Yeah? I hear she's pretty hot."

Willie thought that was putting it mildly. In fact, he couldn't figure out why Marla and Suzanna had bad reputations and Patty didn't. "Listen, she's driving me home, okay?"

"No sweat. I can't wait to hear about this tomorrow."

Willie gave Patty directions to his place. She drove faster than he thought was safe in the snow, but at least she hadn't been drinking, so he didn't say anything about it. Anyway, he didn't want her to think he was some kind of chicken.

When they went past Carol's cabin, he saw something that made him say, "Slow down a minute, will you?"

She put on the brakes, and they skidded across the road, but it was okay, because they didn't hit anything. He looked out the rear window and saw two people building a humongous snowman out in front of Carol's cabin. He didn't see his dad's truck, and he was wondering who it was with Carol when he realized his dad could've easily walked down there.

Which meant that as soon as Willie was out of the house, his dad was sneaking down to see Carol. Except building a snowman didn't fit. Why would his dad sneak out to see her and then build a snowman?

"What're you looking at?" asked Patty; then she turned around and looked in the direction he was looking. "What is that, kids out playing?"

"Yeah, just a couple of kids."

"At this hour?"

Willie shrugged. "You can go now, Patty."

He had her park a little way down the road past his house. He wished he had the nerve to invite her in, but he didn't think that was advisable. He and his dad might not be speaking, but he was pretty sure he'd be in real trouble if his dad came home and found him with Patty, particularly since he had a pretty good idea that Patty didn't always keep her clothes on.

Patty turned out the headlights and cut the engine. "Want to get in the back seat?" she asked him.

Willie couldn't manage more than a gulp.

Chapter Thirteen

It was late afternoon on Christmas Eve when the telegram was delivered to Carol. It was from a Dr. Stein at Bellevue Hospital in New York, and all it said was for her to call.

She couldn't imagine why a doctor in New York would want her to call him. She had no relatives in New York, no friends who would want her called in case of an emergency. Then she thought of Phyllis, her agent, but Phyllis had a husband; surely they wouldn't be calling her.

She drove down to the general store and got there just as they were closing. When she said she needed to make an emergency phone call to New York, they let her in, put the lights back on and gave her change for a twenty for the phone call.

Then she was put on hold by the hospital for a good ten minutes until she thought she was going to run out of change. Finally, a youthful-sounding person came on the phone identifying herself as Dr. Stein.

Carol gave her name and said that she had received a telegram.

"Oh, yes, Ms Jones," said the doctor. "A John Rafferty asked that you be notified."

Carol held her breath, waiting to be told he was dead, but then the doctor was saying, "He's had a heart attack, and we have him in intensive care at the moment."

"Will he be all right?" Carol wanted to know.

"It's too early to say. He's in good physical condition otherwise, but there is his age, of course."

"Tell him I'll be up there as soon as I can," said Carol, then rang off a few moments later.

She thanked the owners for letting her use the phone, then drove directly to Raney's house. She wanted to tell him about Mr. Rafferty and also use his phone to make an airline reservation. She just couldn't be bothered with the fact that she and Raney weren't seeing each other. He knew J.J. far better than she did and would know if he had any relatives who should be notified.

When she got there, though, no one was home, and the truck was gone. They must have left for his parents' house already, which meant they wouldn't be home until late Christmas night.

For the first time, Carol really missed the convenience of a telephone. She tried to think where there was one she could use, then decided to go by Donna Lee's house. She would have to tell her she wouldn't be spending Christmas with her, anyway, and also deliver the pies for their dessert.

"Hi, honey," said Donna Lee at the door, then stopped smiling at the look on Carol's face. "What's the matter?"

Carol explained to her, then used Donna Lee's phone to call every available airline. None had seats on Christmas Eve, which she would have realized if she had been thinking straight.

"I guess I'll have to drive up there," said Carol.

"All by yourself?" Donna Lee sounded horrified.

"I drove down here by myself. Donna Lee, do you know if Mr. Rafferty has any relatives I should call."

Donna Lee shook her head. "Not that I know of. Raney'd know better; he was real close with old J.J."

"Raney's on his way to his folks' house."

"I'll give him a call when he gets back," said Donna Lee. "Let me have your phone number in New York in case he wants to get in touch with you."

Donna Lee wanted her to stay to supper, but Carol wanted to start out as soon as possible. She had to fill up with gas and pack a few things; then she could go. One thing she was thankful for: there wasn't any snow being forecast.

RANEY AND WILLIE made the drive to Raney's parents' house in silence. At least Raney made it in silence; Willie had that headset on his head the whole way.

Raney's dad worked for the railroad and had been transferred a few years back when the trains stopped running through Rock Ridge. His parents hadn't got another house when they moved.

His mother said she was tired of taking care of a big place, and his father usually went along with whatever his wife wanted. So now they had a garden apartment with hardly any upkeep. His dad had taken up golf, and his mom had got her real-estate license and now worked for the first time in her life.

They were both in their fifties and in good health, and sometimes Raney envied them. They not only had a good, solid marriage, but they also seemed to be friends. He thought maybe he'd talk to them about the situation with Carol and see if they had any good advice for him.

His mom got him aside as soon as they got there and told him the puppy, a Labrador, was next door with a neighbor. Ever since Willie had got to the age where he no longer believed in Santa Claus, they opened their presents on Christmas Eve. This, his mom told him, was a great relief to her neighbor, as the puppy wasn't housebroken as yet.

They had a big supper of baked ham as soon as they got there; then Willie and his grandfather watched TV; Raney sat in the kitchen while his mom did the cleaning up. He had offered to help, but she hadn't wanted any.

"Something wrong between you and Willie?" his mom wanted to know even before he got the chance to bring the subject up.

"What makes you ask?" He hadn't thought it was noticeable. With other people around to talk to, their not talking to each other hadn't seemed evident to him.

"You two haven't even looked at each other since you walked in the door."

Raney gave her an abbreviated and expurgated version of the problem, with his mother interrupting him now and then to ask a question.

"You're almost thirty-five years old, Raney, and you're letting a fifteen-year-old lead you around by the nose."

"He hasn't had it easy, what with his mother leaving and all," said Raney.

"He's long got over that. He's just used to getting his own way with you, that's all."

"I'm not all that easy on him; just ask Willie."

"You're a pushover; always were. You shouldn't be letting Willie dictate who you can date and who you can't."

"That's just it, Mom. It's not exactly a dating situation."

"I'm not following your meaning, son."

"I'm not really interested in dating her."

"Well, then what's the problem?"

"I feel like I'm too old for dating. What I'd really like, I think, is to marry her."

His mother turned around from the sink and looked at him, a big smile on her face. "Well, good for you. I was afraid Charlene might've soured you on marriage."

"Carol's different. In fact, she's really different, not like anyone I ever knew."

"Does she feel the same way you do?"

"I haven't a notion. One thing, she's pretty independent."

"I still say, don't let Willie stand in your way. Another few years he'll be off on his own."

"I just can't feature being married to a woman my son's in love with. You really don't see problems with that?"

Lou Catlin laughed out loud. "Sounds like one of those soap operas."

"Now you see what I mean."

"Listen, Raney—there's one thing I know about teenage love. It might be strong as all get out, but it usually doesn't last long. Kids just don't have long attention spans. Particularly if the love's unrequited."

"So what you're saying is, give it some time."

She nodded.

Raney sighed. He knew she was right; it was just that he was already getting tired of waiting. Just knowing she was only down the road from him but for all intents and purposes could be thousands of miles away was driving him crazy.

"I'm hoping the puppy will soften him up."

"Well, it sure is adorable, Raney. I swear, if I don't hear Willie thanking you for her, I'm going to keep her myself."

It was about ten o'clock when they started opening their gifts. First Raney and Willie exchanged presents with Willie's grandparents. Raney had picked them out and included Willie's name on the cards. He had bought his dad a nice cardigan sweater and several dozen golf balls, and his dad right away tried on the sweater and said it was perfect.

For his mom he had got a gold chain with a charm on the end. The charm was a miniature Sold sign, and his mom said she loved it and that everyone at the real-estate office was going to be jealous. Raney had thought of her the minute he saw it.

His folks had always given him clothes. This year Raney got a good-looking jacket that looked like real leather that would be perfect for work, and Willie got a wool sweater and two shirts. Usually, Willie was hard put to show any enthusiasm for clothes, but for some reason he really seemed to like what he got this time. It made Raney wonder if maybe Willie was out to impress Carol with his clothes. Then he remembered he wasn't seeing Carol anymore.

Raney decided to hell with not speaking at Christmas and said to Willie, "Your present's a little unusual this year, but I hope you'll like it," then looked at his mother. She told them she'd be right back, then left the room, and Raney heard the front door open and close.

"It's outside?" said Willie to no one in particular.

"That's right," said Raney.

"It can't be a car 'cause I'm not old enough to drive."

"Couldn't afford a car, anyway," said Raney, realizing that even though both of them were talking into the air, at least they were communicating.

When his mom came back with the puppy in her arms and handed it right over to Willie, the boy's jaw practically fell off its hinge. The puppy, a little squirming ball of black, immediately wet all over Willie, who thought that was hilarious.

"Going to be a good hunting dog, that one," said Raney's dad. "Be sure you start training it early."

"What're you going to name her?" asked his mom.

Willie was flat on the floor now, and the puppy was tugging at his hair with her teeth. "I think I'll name her Aunt Lolly."

Raney nearly fell out of the chair when he heard that one. Then his mother asked, "Where'd you ever come up with a name like that?"

Willie grinned up at her. "Dad and I know this lady who draws these greeting cards. She does ones of this character called Aunt Lolly, this really funny old lady. Anyway, I kind of like the name. I can always shorten it to just Lolly." He put his face down next to the puppy's and said, "Hey, Lolly, do you like that name?" When the puppy licked his nose, everyone laughed.

Raney caught his mom giving him a questioning look, and he just shrugged. He sure as hell couldn't figure out why Willie had brought up Carol.

He had to think it was a good sign, though.

Then Willie reached into his pocket and handed Raney a small, flat package. Raney opened it up, and it was a pocket calculator about the size of a credit card.

"Thanks. This is sure going to come in handy," said Raney.

"I figured you could use it for work," said Willie.

"I sure can. Also to balance my checking account. I didn't know they made these things so small."

"It fits right in your wallet," Willie told him.

Raney didn't know whether it was because of the puppy or because of Christmas or because his parents were there, but whatever the reason, he was glad Willie was talking to him.

And he sure seemed taken with the puppy.

IT WAS EARLY EVENING when Carol reached New York. Traffic was light, and she headed straight for the hospital. Dr. Stein wasn't on duty, but she had left word that Carol could visit Mr. Rafferty even if it wasn't during regular visiting hours.

He was in a semiprivate room, and the other occupant had a curtain pulled around the bed. Carol took a chair next to Mr. Rafferty's bed and waited for the man to open his eyes.

When he did, he managed a crooked smile and said, "What day is it?"

Carol smiled back. "Merry Christmas."

"I didn't mean to drag you back to New York."

"That's okay. All I was going to do was have dinner at Donna Lee's."

"You friends with Donna Lee?"

Carol nodded. "She's a good person."

"That she is," said J.J. "Her grandfather was my best friend when we were young."

"How've you been enjoying New York?"

"I've been like a kid in a candy shop. I've been to most of the plays, dozens of bookstores and all of the museums."

"In this short a time?"

J.J. chuckled. "At my age, time's something you can't waste."

"I read your books," Carol told him. "I didn't think I'd like them so much." Then she went on to tell him how one of his characters had given her the idea for her Aunt Lolly cards.

"Funny where ideas come from, isn't it?" J. J. asked her, and she nodded. "I've written some since I've been up here."

"I can see why you didn't stay in New York. I've got tons of work done down there."

"Haven't been bored to death, have you?"

"Not bored to death but a little lonely sometimes."

"Good-looking girl like you oughtn't to be lonely."

Carol thought of telling him about Raney, then decided not to. She felt that someone recovering from a heart attack ought to hear only good news.

She did tell him about the electric heaters and electric blanket and the blackout, though, and got a good laugh out of him. Then she worried that maybe he wasn't supposed to be laughing.

"So you like it in Rock Ridge, do you?"

"Very much. And I love your cabin."

He gave a deep sigh. "I was kinda hoping you'd say you hated it."

She gave him a questioning look.

"It's just that—Oh, hell, there's no way to say it but just straight out. I don't know how much longer I have, Carol, but I'd like to spend what time there is back home."

Carol realized she should have expected that, only she hadn't. "You mean you want your cabin back?"

"I know it's highly unfair. We had an agreement."

"No, that's all right. I understand," she said, thinking that she might not ever see Raney again.

"If you like it down there all that much, there're plenty of places you could rent cheap.

But they wouldn't be the same as her cabin down the road from Raney. Still, her leaving might turn out to be the best solution. It was so frustrating living so close to him and not being able to see him.

"How'd you get here, fly?"

"No, I couldn't get a flight. I drove up."

"No wonder you look exhausted. Been driving since yesterday?"

"I didn't mind; I like driving at night."

"Run along home and get some rest."

"I'll be back tomorrow to see you. Can I bring you anything?"

"If you could bring my shaving kit, it's in the bathroom."

She nodded.

"And maybe my pipe."

"Are you supposed to be smoking?"

"You really think it matters?"

Carol leaned over the bed and gave him a kiss before she left. He was such a nice man; she wished she had got a chance to get to know him better.

She drove home, parked her car in the garage under her building, then took the elevator up to her apartment. She felt her first sense of culture shock when she entered her apartment. It seemed like so much space after the small cabin. She had thought it might look different, as J.J.'s cabin would look different to him with all her additions, but the only clues to J.J.'s living there were some clothes in the bedroom and a pile of library books by the bed.

For some reason she felt too hyper to go to sleep, so she made herself some tea and then called her agent at home to wish her a merry Christmas. She told her why she was in the city, and they made plans to have lunch together the following day.

She called some friends who she knew would be alone for Christmas, and they got caught up on news; then she placed a long-distance call to her oldest brother's house in Evanston where she knew all her brothers would be gathering for Christmas.

She spent almost an hour talking to everyone there; then, after hanging up, she couldn't think of anyone else to call. She couldn't even remember liking talking on the phone when she had one all the time; now she couldn't seem to get enough of it.

Or maybe it was just that she didn't want to be alone with her thoughts. The thing was, she wasn't ready to leave Rock Ridge yet. She had hoped to be there in the spring to see the woods behind her cabin come to life, and she had hoped to do some fishing in the summer.

And she had also hoped that somehow things would right themselves and she and Raney could go on from where they had left off. But even if she hadn't met Raney, she still wouldn't have been ready to return to New York. Even though she could appreciate her roomy apartment and the use of a phone, the city had lost all appeal for her.

She was also tired of living alone. She had begun to think she would always be alone, had even felt acceptance for the idea, but that had been before she had fallen in love with Raney Catlin. She knew that in a way he reminded her of her father, but not in any way that should send her running to the nearest shrink. It was just that he was interested in the same things her father had interested her in, the kinds of things the men she had met in New York were never interested in.

She knew that once he got accustomed to a woman who liked the same things he did, they would grow to be friends as well as lovers. And she knew she would be good for Willie once he got over his crush on her. The boy seemed to need someone to confide in desperately, someone with whom he could discuss dreams and aspirations. He was an intelligent boy, too intelligent to quit school after high school and take any job he could get.

Great. So she was perfect for both of them; that still didn't solve anything. Now she would be in New York, and they would be in Rock Ridge, and she might as well try to start forgetting them and get on with her life.

WILLIE HAD AUNT LOLLY inside his jacket with her head poking out on the drive home. He had always wanted a dog. Always. He couldn't believe his dad had actually got him one. Without even remembering that he wasn't going to talk to his dad on the way back, he said, "What made you get me a dog?"

There was a long silence; then his dad said, "It was Carol's idea."

Willie couldn't think of a thing to say to that. He didn't think his dad was going to say anything else, either, but then he said, "I love you, kid. I love you, but I love her, too. What're we going to do about it?"

Willie felt like the worst kind of creep. He felt so stupid now to have made that big scene about Carol. But he couldn't very well say, "Hey, Dad, forget about it. I'm in love with someone else now." Because if he said that, then he'd look like a real jerk who couldn't make up his mind whom he loved or something. And he would've made his dad miserable and Carol miserable for no reason.

He knew they had been miserable, too. He had seen the way they looked at each other the day of the blackout. He had seen them hugging in the kitchen when they thought he was still upstairs. And he had seen them playing like two kids in the snow, building that snowman. They were really good together, and because of him they weren't even seeing each other.

But he couldn't just say, "Listen, it was all a mistake." For one thing, his dad would probably kill him, or at least lose all respect for him.

He couldn't wait to show Patty the puppy. Patty had got him a Christmas present. He hadn't known whether they were going together or not, so he hadn't got her anything, but she had bought him one of Bruce Springsteen's cassettes for his Walkman. She said Bruce Springsteen's music really turned her on.

He could hardly believe his luck, but just about everything turned Patty on. He had trouble believing she was even interested in him, but she told him he was very mature for his age and a good conversationalist. Which kind of surprised him, because whenever they were together, they didn't talk all that much.

He sneaked a look at his dad and saw the dejected look on his face. He figured he ought to try to cheer him up, so he said, "This is the best Christmas present I ever got."

"I'll help you train her. She comes from a good line of hunting dogs."

"That'd be great."

He couldn't think of anything to say after that, though, so they drove the rest of the way in silence.

The phone was ringing when they let themselves in the house, and thinking it might be Patty, Willie ran to answer it. It wasn't, though; it was Donna Lee for his dad.

As soon as he hung up, his dad said, "We're going to New York."

Willie just stared at him in astonishment.

"J.J. had a heart attack. Carol drove up there, but she shouldn't have to handle it alone. We're the closest thing to relatives J.J.'s got."

Willie knew one thing: he didn't want to go away. If he left, Patty might start going with someone else. "Why can't I stay here, Dad?" he asked, thinking that he and Patty would have the house all to themselves.

"You're coming with me."

"Why? Why do I have to go?"

His dad gave him a strange look. "What I can't figure, son, is why all of a sudden you're so anxious to throw me and Carol together?"

Willie thought fast. "But the puppy. Someone has to be here to take care of the puppy."

But his dad was already calling the airlines and making reservations for the next morning, then asking about taking a dog along. "No problem," he told Willie when he had hung up. "She's small enough to fit under the seat. You'll just have to find some kind of box for her and punch holes in it."

Willie couldn't think of any more excuses. When his dad left the room, he called Patty.

"How was your Christmas?" she asked him first thing.

"Fine, Patty; in fact, great. I got a puppy."

"When do I get to see it?"

"The thing is, I have to fly to New York tomorrow."

He heard an intake of breath, then, "Are you kidding me, Willie Catlin?"

"I tried to get out of it, but—"

"Tried to get out of going to New York? I'd die to go to New York. Oh, you're so lucky I can't stand it!"

He began to relax, picturing himself as the world traveler. Come to think of it, he didn't know anyone who had ever been to New York. "Want me to bring you anything from the big city?"

"Oh, Willie, would you? Would you bring me a T-shirt that says New York?"

"Sure," he said, thinking that would make up for not having got her a Christmas present. "I'll give you a call from there, too."

"Don't waste your money on that, Willie. But send me some postcards, okay?"

Willie was beginning to think New York wasn't such a bad idea. He'd never flown in a jet before, either. And maybe when he got there, he'd figure out some way to get his dad and Carol back together.

SHE WAS SOAKING in the bathtub, another luxury she had missed in Rock Ridge, when the phone rang. Since it was midnight and everyone who knew she was in

New York she had already spoken to, she figured it was probably a wrong number and ignored it.

Then, when it stopped ringing, she started to worry that it had been the hospital. She was just putting on her robe and was going to call Bellevue when the phone rang again. She sat down on the bed and prepared herself for the worst, then picked up the bedroom extension.

"Carol? You just get in from the hospital?"

She found herself holding her breath in wonder that it was Raney.

"Carol? You there?"

"Was that you before? I was in the bathtub."

She heard him sigh. "Donna Lee just told me. We're flying to New York tomorrow."

"You and Willie?"

"J.J.'s not your problem, Carol. How is he, anyway?"

"I'm not sure. He seemed pretty good, but I won't be able to talk to his doctor until tomorrow. The thing is, he wants to return to Rock Ridge."

"Don't blame him. I wouldn't want to be laid up in a strange city."

"I was thinking I'd drive him back down there as soon as the doctor says he can be moved."

"We'll come along with you."

"Raney, are you sure that's a good idea? What about Willie?"

"As far as I'm concerned, he can stop acting like a spoiled kid. He's got to learn he can't have everything his way."

"What you're doing is putting me in a difficult position."

"Let's see what happens when we get there. By the way, nobody knows your address. Want to give it to me?"

She did, and then he read it back to her, and at the very end he said, "By the way, darlin', I love you."

"What?" said Carol, totally taken by surprise.

"You heard me. See you tomorrow," he said. Then he hung up before she could tell him she loved him, too. But she was pretty sure he already knew. He just wasn't the type to tell her otherwise.

The only trouble was, now she was definitely too excited to sleep.

Chapter Fourteen

They took a taxi from the airport. When they got out, Raney looked up at the building Carol lived in. It looked very large and very impressive, and just as impressive was the doorman who opened the door for them and the way the man had to call up to see if they were expected.

The elevator was as big as his bathroom at home and much more elegant, and he could see Willie's eyes widening at the speed of the ascent. Then the puppy made a whimpering noise, and Willie took it out of its box and held it.

The Mercedes should have prepared him for her building, and the building should have prepared him for her apartment, but it hadn't. Happy as he was to see her when she opened the door to them, his eyes couldn't help going past her and then focusing on the view from her living-room windows.

"That's some view you've got," he said, then instantly cursed himself for sounding like some country hick. Which, as a matter of fact, he probably was. At least he would be to a New Yorker.

"Come out and see it from the terrace," said Carol, sounding to him like a tour guide.

They still hadn't properly said hello or anything, but they were following her through French doors and out onto a terrace that looked as if it overlooked the entire city and must have been big enough to hold a few hundred people comfortably.

Willie went right over to the stone wall surrounding it and leaned over, looking down. Raney found himself staying a distance away. He didn't think it was going to collapse—it looked too solid for that—but you never knew.

After they'd looked around for a couple of minutes, Carol said, "Come on inside; it's cold out here. Anyway, I want to see that puppy you're holding, Willie."

"I named her Aunt Lolly," Willie told her.

Carol looked from Willie to Raney, and he shrugged. "Better warn her she's not housebroken," he said to Willie.

"Don't worry about that," said Carol. "I like dogs better than I like carpeting."

Which right away made Raney notice the carpeting. It was a wheat color and as thick as molasses. Somehow he had pictured her apartment being yellow, probably because of the yellow touches in the cabin. But it was all in neutral colors: white walls, off-white carpeting, the furniture a light wood and the upholstery all in white. In fact, the only color at all was in the pictures on the wall, and that's about all they were, just big splashes of color.

And every damn thing in the whole place looked expensive.

Carol disappeared for a minute, then returned with a bowl of water for the puppy that she just set in the middle of the nice carpeting. "Can I get you two something to drink?" she asked them.

"I'll have a Coke," said Willie, and he watched as they seemed to find that amusing.

"How about you?" Carol asked Raney. "I don't have Jack Daniel's, but I have just about everything else."

"I'll have a beer, if you have it."

She disappeared again, and this time Willie followed her, so Raney went along for the ride. Her kitchen wasn't half as large as his own, but it was outfitted with every appliance known to man plus a few he didn't recognize. He saw that there was another door off the kitchen that led to the terrace.

Carol handed him a bottle of imported beer, took one for herself, then said, "Would you like to see the rest of the place?"

Raney didn't really want to. What he wanted to do was take her in his arms, but for some reason he was beginning to feel a little ill at ease with her. Not so Willie, who kept saying how neat everything was. Only he didn't mean tidy.

She took them down a hall and into a large room where she did her work. One whole wall held her cards, all framed, and another was bookshelves filled with art materials. There was even a bed in there, and Carol told Willie he could sleep in this room.

"We can get a hotel room," said Raney.

"I have plenty of room," she said, then led them farther down the hall to her own bedroom. She had a king-size bed, which unaccountably annoyed him, and the room was done in browns with touches of pumpkin. He had seen the TV and stereo in the living room, and there were duplicates in the bedroom.

When they got back to the living room, Carol said, "The couch here makes into a bed. If it's not comfortable, Raney, I'll sleep out here, and you can have the bedroom."

"I can sleep anywhere," he told her, though he would have preferred sleeping with her. Which made him wonder why he had insisted that Willie come along with him. No, he didn't really wonder. He had to get things straightened out with Willie first.

Anyhow, now that he saw how she lived, he couldn't imagine that she would be the least bit interested in marrying him. He didn't know why it hadn't occurred to him before that she probably made ten times more money than he did. Maybe a hundred times, for all he knew.

He should've known the first time he saw that new Mercedes of hers. For some reason, though, he had figured that was all she had. He was so used to seeing her in those funny clothes she wore that looked secondhand for the most part, and then she had been living in J.J.'s little cabin. With his house, he had felt positively rich by comparison.

Even though he wasn't conversant with New York prices, he figured the rent on her apartment had to be more a month than his mortgage payments were for a full year. He just had never thought drawing pictures for greeting cards could pay so well.

Sure, Raney, he told himself, *she's really going to want to give all this up just to live with some country boy in Rock Ridge, Georgia.*

He finally remembered his reason for being there. "How's J.J.?" he asked her.

Carol gave a smile of relief. "He's doing fine. The doctor told him he's going to have to take it easier from now on and cut down on the smoking and drinking, but she says there's no reason why he can't live to be a hundred if he's careful."

"That's good news," said Raney.

"He can leave the hospital in another couple of days, and I'm driving him back to Georgia."

"We'll go with you," said Raney, and saw Willie give him a surprised look.

"Four of us and a dog?" asked Willie.

"We'll manage," Raney told him.

Carol said that they could go over and see J.J. in the hospital; then Willie said, "Could I look around the city a little on my own while you go up there?"

Raney was about to say no way, the place was too dangerous, but Carol was already saying, "Sure, go ahead. The best way to learn your way around is just to go out and start walking. Most of the streets in Manhattan are numbered, so it's pretty easy, but if you get lost, just ask directions."

"What about Lolly?" Willie wanted to know.

Carol said, "I think it's a little cold out for a puppy. Why don't you put some newspapers down in the kitchen and lock her in there? And you better pick up some puppy food while you're out.''

''Thanks, Carol,'' said Willie, leaving Raney to wonder if all was forgiven or if Willie had some new plan up his sleeve.

WILLIE WAS SO EXCITED at being in New York he wasn't even missing Patty yet. What he was also finding exciting was the way Carol lived. She must really have the bucks to live in a place like this.

He wondered if there was any possibility of his dad marrying her. It wouldn't be half bad to have a stepmother with a Mercedes and a stereo system worth a couple of thou and probably enough money in the bank to travel around the world if she wanted to.

Not that he wouldn't like her just as much if she were poor. She was a really nice person and had never, not even for a minute, treated him like a kid. He knew his dad would've said no to his going out into the city by himself, but Carol figured he was old enough to take care of himself. He hoped they did get married; maybe his dad would go back to being less strict with him.

And he'd sure like to talk to Carol about Patty. There were just some things you couldn't talk to your dad about, because you didn't want to end up sounding stupid. But with Carol he never felt stupid.

Except why would someone like Carol even want to marry his dad? With her money, she ought to be able to marry anyone.

AFTER VISITING J.J., Carol took Raney on a quick tour of Manhattan, pointing out to him some of her favorite spots.

"It's a beautiful city," Raney said.

"That's because it's decorated for Christmas. It's the prettiest time in New York."

"I guess you really love it here."

She pulled up to a red light and looked over at him. "I used to. It seems to have lost its magic for me." That was his cue to say, "Then leave it all and live with me in Rock Ridge," but he didn't. In fact, he was acting decidedly strange.

When they got back to her apartment, she made them each a drink, then said, "Want to order in some Chinese? That's one thing I've really missed."

"What else have you missed?" he asked her.

She didn't even have to think about that. "A telephone and a bathtub."

That got a chuckle out of him. "Well, some of us have those things in Rock Ridge."

Willie came in then, and for a good twenty minutes they were entertained by his adventures in the city. He ended up with, "I wouldn't mind living here."

"You can live where you want when you're eighteen," Raney told him, and Carol was thinking that maybe Willie could go to college in New York.

"Hey, Carol, could I use your phone?" Willie asked.

"Sure. If you want some privacy, there are phones in the bedrooms."

"Who're you calling, son?"

Willie looked flustered. "I promised Patty I'd call her."

Carol and Raney exchanged glances; then Raney said, "I don't recall hearing about any Patty."

Willie was desperately avoiding their eyes when he said, "She's just a girl I've been seeing."

There was a decidedly pregnant silence; then Carol said, "Gee, Willie, and here I thought you were in love with me." She could see that Raney almost died when she said that, but she thought it was time for some shock tactics.

Willie turned a deep shade of red. "I do love you, Carol. As a person, you know? I mean, I think you're one of my best friends."

She wasn't going to let him off that easily, not after all he'd put her and Raney through. "That's not the way I remember it." She looked over at Raney and saw he was beginning to enjoy it.

Willie said, "Okay, so I was stupid. Is that what you want me to say? Look, I did think I loved you like a girlfriend, but that was before I met Patty."

"Does this mean you don't mind my seeing your father." Carol persisted.

"Mind? I think it's great. In fact, I think you ought to let me fly back with J.J. and you two drive back and maybe get married along the way."

That was more than Carol had counted on. "Uh, I think you can go make that phone call now, Willie."

But Willie just stood there, grinning at her. "Not until I hear how this turns out."

"Leave us alone, Willie." Raney's tone brooked no argument.

With a mischevous look at his father, Willie left the room. Carol waited until she heard a door close, then said, "You have quite an imaginative son."

"Not all that imaginative. I'll bet I thought of it first."

Things were going too fast for her. "Thought of what first?"

"Marrying you. That was before I saw your setup here, though. Now I figure, what do you need me for?"

"Are you serious?"

"Perfectly serious. Hell, darlin', you look like you could buy and sell me ten times over."

She could feel herself grinning. "My money some kind of threat to your ego, Raney?"

"Not me, darlin'. I got nothing against rich women."

"But you wouldn't marry one."

Now he was grinning. "Who said I wouldn't marry one? I just might retire and spend all my time fishing. That'd sure be the life."

"Well, I might just retire and go fishing with you. Then who would pay the bills?"

"You like to fish?"

"Damn right I like to fish."

"Then I guess I'm going to have to marry you. Spent all my life trying to find a woman who liked to fish."

"If that was a proposal, Raney, it left a lot to be desired." But she was loving it.

"It wasn't a proposal. When I propose, you'll know it, darlin'. And there's just one thing that's standing in my way."

"And what would that be?"

His eyes went past her. "Am I correct in assuming that that contraption is one of those giant TV screens? The kind they have in bars?"

"I like watching football on a big screen."

"I'd marry you just to get my hands on that."

Carol folded her arms across her chest. "I don't imagine that was a proposal, either, was it?"

"Nope, but here it comes. Will you marry me, darlin'?"

"I guess so, but only because I want to be Willie's stepmother."

"I guess I deserved that," said Raney.

"I guess you did."